"Ma'am. M...

Clint swept the hat off his head and held his breath as he witnessed Sonya's startled amber eyes narrow in speculation. Would his gamble pay off, or would she toss him out with a snap of her slim fingers?

She laughed. "Is that a fact? *You're* my Rocky Ridge man, are you?"

Clint winked. "Look no further, ma'am."

"Oh, but I'll have to take a closer look, a much closer look." She inched past the boundary of his personal comfort zone. "I have to ensure you possess all of the...ah...attributes I need."

"I've never had any complaints about my attributes before now." The woman held his future in the palm of her hand. He was at her mercy. But he'd be damned if he'd let her see that.

She raised one eyebrow. "Perhaps their standards aren't as high as mine."

"Well, you just haul out your yardstick and we'll see how I measure up."

A smile graced her lips. "Somehow, I doubt I'd need a stick that long."

"Ah, but you haven't seen the extent of my hidden qualities."

Sonya leaned closer. "By the time I'm finished with you, cowboy, you won't have anything left to hide."

His voice was husky when he replied, "Is that a promise?"

Dear Reader,

Isn't it an incredible thrill when dreams finally come true?

Writing *The Rocky Ridge Man* was a culmination of a dream I've nurtured for years, and I'm delighted it's my debut novel for Temptation.

In creating the story and the characters' backgrounds, I drew upon the experience I gained while employed as writer/producer of television commercials in Moncton, New Brunswick. Although, believe me, I *never* had the opportunity to search for the best derriere in the East (or West)!

I also relied on my wonderful memories of the year I spent in Banff, Alberta, in the heart of the Rocky Mountains.

As my very first book, *The Rocky Ridge Man* and its characters will always occupy a special place in my heart. I hope you enjoy reading Sonya and Clint's story as much as I enjoyed writing it. I'd love to hear from you. Please write to me with an SASE at: P.O. Box 1231, Moncton, New Brunswick, E1C 8P9, Canada.

Regards,

Meredith March

THE ROCKY RIDGE MAN
Meredith March

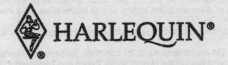

TORONTO • NEW YORK • LONDON
AMSTERDAM • PARIS • SYDNEY • HAMBURG
STOCKHOLM • ATHENS • TOKYO • MILAN • MADRID
PRAGUE • WARSAW • BUDAPEST • AUCKLAND

I'm indebted to Cheryl Leger, Georgie Phillips,
Lorraine Coyle and Ruth MacLean for their unflagging
encouragement and support.
Thanks to Pam Hopkins and Susan Sheppard for their guidance,
and to Tory LeBlanc, Julianne MacLean and Jackie Manning.
My love to the three most important people in my life—
Steven, Alexander and Jenifer Anne for their support,
understanding and love.

A special thank-you to Harrison Ford for
his words of encouragement delivered
via an interview with Barbara Walters:
The force is within you. Force yourself.
I did.

ISBN 0-373-25843-7

THE ROCKY RIDGE MAN

1

TWENTY MALE DERRIERES stood at attention, buns squeezed rigid, awaiting her next command.

Stifling a groan, Sonya Duncan squared her aching shoulders and scrutinized the lineup of spandex-stuffed, cotton-crushed or denim-bound glutei maximi. Three days of scheduled auditions with models from Alberta's best agencies had given way to another two days of open auditions from Calgary's male population, and she still hadn't found what she was looking for—one perfect set of masculine buns.

"Mmm. Don't you just love these cattle calls?" Neil's reedy voice murmured close to her ear. "I never dreamed Calgary would have so much...beefcake." He sighed gustily as he handed her an untidy pile of photos.

"This isn't a dream. It's a nightmare," Sonya muttered under her breath as she spilled the collage of disparate candidates onto her clipboard and rescanned the lineup. "Looks like most of them have indulged in too much beef or cake. Or they have no butt at all."

"Guess we're really scraping the *bottom* of the barrel," Neil replied cheerfully, nudging her in the arm. "Get it? Bottom..." He convulsed with laughter.

A smile tugged at Sonya's mouth. Neil's quick wit was one of the reasons she'd chosen him as her assistant. He excelled at schmoozing with the clients, which allowed her to concentrate on the job at hand. Speaking of which...

Sonya cleared her throat. "Okay, gentlemen. Please face the lights once more." While they complied, she glanced sideways at her petite associate. As usual, Neil was dressed in his trademark skintight black pants and black T-shirt; this one had a giant scarlet imprint of a pair of lips. She watched as he ogled one of the more handsome models—a dark-haired Latin type with bulging muscles and liquid eyes. The model tossed Neil a brilliant smile and a not-so-subtle wink.

"Thank you, gentlemen." Sonya struggled to keep the fatigue out of her voice. "We appreciate your patience. Would you and you—" she gestured to a well-proportioned blonde and a rangy man with dark, curly hair "—please report to Karen at the desk outside the studio door? The rest of you are free to go. Thank you." She noticed Mr. Liquid Eyes deliberately lingered behind the others, trying to catch Neil's attention.

Sonya raised an eyebrow. "Friend of yours?"

"Not yet." Her assistant sized the other man up. "But I think women would drool over those muscles of his." Neil slid his gaze to her. "Don't you think he'd make the perfect Rocky Ridge man?"

Cocking her head, Sonya quickly sized up the man's physique. "Maybe if our client wanted to sell jockstraps instead of blue jeans. We need someone with less...brawn. Your friend's look is too Neanderthal. I see the Rocky Ridge man as more sophisticated. And, proportionally, this guy's legs are too short for his body. Not exactly what we're looking for, but he'd be okay in a head and shoulders shot for male cosmetics products. Make sure you put his photo in our active file."

Neil gave her an exasperated look. "Forget the specifications, sweetie. Where does he rate on the pitter-patter scale?"

Sonya frowned. "The what?"

"You know. Pitter-patter, sex appeal, sweaty palms and a racing heart?" Neil feigned surprise. "You *do* have a heart, don't you?"

Her libido, or lack of it, wasn't up for discussion. She half grimaced, half smiled at him. "I must. Otherwise I'd fire you for prolonging an already exhausting day."

"Oookaay. Time for the subservient mode." Neil snapped to attention, clicking his heels together. "Is there anything I can do for you, *mon commandant*? Your wish is my command." He followed her as she returned to her worktable in the middle of the large studio.

Sonya collapsed in her chair and shuffled a huge stack of photos, putting the day's rejects into a bulging folder and securing the few remaining ones beneath the metal clasp of her clipboard. Then she opened her project binder. "Neil, can you tell everyone to take ten? My feet are killing me."

Saluting, Neil switched on his headset and, with great animation, relayed her instructions.

No doubt about it, Neil was flamboyant, but he was one of the best art directors in the business. That's why she'd enticed, threatened and wheedled until he'd finally given in and agreed to leave Mecca, as he called Toronto, and accompany her to "the uncivilized Wild West."

Sonya slipped off a high-heeled shoe and massaged her aching arch. She relied on Neil's expertise to help her design and implement the perfect campaign for Rocky Ridge blue jeans. After all, Zenith Communications' president, Lawrence MacLeod, had made it clear her bid for the vice presidency hinged on her performance in opening the Calgary office. And Sonya wasn't prepared to accept failure; she'd worked too hard over the past six years to falter now. Especially after the Saunders' catastrophe. It had been a painful lesson; personal favors often came with strings attached. Because she couldn't afford a repeat performance of that mess, she now stuck to her cardinal rule: emotional obligations had no place in business.

Even the dual demands of supervising the setup of a new office, plus mounting a major campaign for a brand-new client, in unfamiliar territory, wouldn't prevent her from reaching her goal. That's why she'd personally selected her team and double-checked the booking of the equipment and facilities. Everything was in place, as she'd arranged, except for one elusive and essential element: the man whose masculine buns would fill his Rocky Ridge blue jeans to perfection.

"Got you some orange juice."

Sonya smiled in thanks as she opened the can and let the cool liquid slide down her parched throat. Sitting back, she tapped a pen against her project schedule. She'd planned this project down to the last minute and the last dollar. In this business, there was no room for costly errors. "Neil, how many do we have on the call-back list?"

"Including the two you just indicated, eight."

Sonya bounced the barrel of the pen against her fingers. "How many more groups to go?"

Neil consulted his clipboard. "One."

Her stomach clenched. "That's all?" The pen dropped from her hand. "We're scheduled to start shooting the billboard ads a week from Monday."

"Maybe you should delay the shoot, continue the search."

Sonya ran her hand through her hair. "That means we'd incur extra costs. I've budgeted for an emergency reserve fund, but it isn't to be utilized for routine production expenses." If she dipped into it now, would there be enough to cover the countless unforeseen expenditures?

Neil snapped his fingers. "What if you choose the best and really work with him, to bring him up to scratch?"

"Good idea, but it would take too much time to mold raw talent. We need someone seasoned, but with limited exposure." Sonya gnawed her lower lip.

"It's hard to believe that out of the three hundred or so we've auditioned, there're only eight possibilities for the Rocky Ridge man."

Sonya flipped through the photos clasped on her clipboard. "Eight lukewarm possibilities." She sighed. "There's no other choice. The whole media campaign's designed around having the right Rocky Ridge look. We'll have to continue the search and try to minimize any repercussions to the project." *And to her bid for the vice presidency.*

Neil's headset crackled. When he turned to her, his blue eyes were worried. "Guess who's just arrived?" He didn't wait for her reply. "Harvey Wilson and Lawrence MacLeod."

Dread wormed about in the pit of Sonya's stomach. She exhaled slowly. "Just what I need." She slipped her shoe firmly onto her foot.

"What's Mr. MacLeod doing here?"

Sonya pasted a smile on her lips. "Apparently our CEO is a good friend of our client. And since Mr. Wilson's contract stipulated he approve our choice of the model, I assume they've both decided to personally view the final selection."

"What are we going to do?"

What, indeed? Normally the client would wait to be presented with the agency's choice. But, of course, Lawrence had a copy of her detailed schedule. "Invite them to sit in. Or if they want, have someone serve them drinks in the boardroom."

Neil relayed the instructions into his headset, then looked her in the eye. "They'd like to watch the final group." He switched off his microphone. "What are you going to do?"

"What I get paid for." Sonya tossed her empty juice can into the metal wastebasket. "Meanwhile, pray that by some miracle we discover our Rocky Ridge man in the final group."

THE STUDIO LIGHTS BRANDED his flesh, just as the summer sunshine had only moments earlier. Clint Silver tugged the brim of his Stetson lower, hunched his shoulders and slid his hands into his jeans pockets.

He was here on a fool's mission. If he succeeded, he'd not only lose all his self-respect, he'd also prove himself the biggest hypocrite in western Canada. Yet if he failed, he'd lose everything.

Impulse, desperation and an ad in a two-day-old newspaper had driven him from an Eighth Avenue coffee shop to this television studio. It was more than a long shot. It was his only shot.

Clint examined the strange assortment of men milling around him. There were a few business types in suits and ties, a number of jocks in various styles of athletic attire, a long-haired hippie in a neon T-shirt and plaid shorts, and a few gangly youths who hadn't quite made it past the final stages of acne. But they all had one thing in common: each sought fame, approval, or perhaps just simple acknowledgment of their physical appearance. All except him. He needed cash.

"Good afternoon, gentlemen. I'm Sonya Duncan, a senior account executive with Zenith Communications. Thank you for taking time to answer our newspaper ad. Today, we are conducting a search for a male model who will epitomize the rugged quality of Rocky Ridge blue jeans."

The cultured voice that issued from beyond the blinding lights was brisk and impersonal. Just like his banker's. The kind of voice that dismissed dreams and destroyed lives, without a second thought.

"We're screening for a specific body type and a certain look. Those who make it past the preliminary screening will return for a further audition, immediately following this session."

What if he didn't make it? Anxiety cramped Clint's heart. He wasn't used to relying on the whims of others to determine his fate. He'd always applied his own skills, pushing the limits of his endurance to achieve his goals. But sometimes that wasn't enough. Hadn't he given all that, and more, to the ranch? Yet he was on the brink of losing it. And he had no time or opportunities to raise the money by any other means. He had to get this job, as much as it revolted him....

"Please form a single line. My assistant, Neil, will gather your photos and résumés."

Clint dug into his pocket and retrieved the black-and-white strip that the photo booth had spit out in exchange for a dollar. The expressions that contorted his frozen images looked more like symptoms of constipation than attempts at a smile. The photos were a far cry from the professional shots that Kristin had once displayed in her portfolio, but would have to do. Kristin. In his grief, he'd burned her portfolio, pictures and all; in the end, they'd been nothing but false memories of a well-packaged ambition. But he couldn't burn from his mind the last image of her ravaged face, etched prematurely by death.

"Excuse me."

Clint glanced at the trim man dressed in a white polo shirt and pleated white shorts who posed beside him. With his slicked-back hair, the guy looked like he'd just bounced in from the tennis court. "Yeah?"

"Don't I know you from somewhere?"

Blood pummeled Clint's heart. This was the last thing he'd expected. "Nope, don't think so." He ignored the other's searching gaze and pretended to examine the strip of photos for his most flattering shot.

"Name's Wesley, Wesley Tanner."

"Mmm."

Wesley waited, but when Clint didn't respond in kind, he cleared his throat. "You do any windsurfing?"

"Nope."

Wesley snapped his fingers. "Skiing?"

Clint's blood pounded in his ears. "A little bit. Years ago."

"The Calgary Olympics! Right?"

Clint's stomach plummeted. Dammit. He hated lying—there'd been too much of it in the past—but in this case he had no choice. He couldn't take a chance on anyone making the connection between him and Kristin. "Sorry. You must have me mixed up with someone else." He forced his lips to curve in what he hoped was an approximation of a smile. With his peripheral vision, he saw the other man's narrow shoulders shrug.

Wesley fingered his close-shaven chin. "Huh. Swear you're a dead ringer for this downhill skier that used to compete for the States. Talk about a daredevil! Watched him ski in the Olympics, just outside Banff. The speed he was going, he would have won the race. Except he crashed into a fence halfway down the course." Wesley shook his head. "Talk about the mother of all wipeouts! The guy's ski pole ripped half his side away."

Clint schooled his face to reveal nothing.

"What an awful mess, blood everywhere. I was the only one on the ski patrol that didn't woof my cookies."

"Ooohh. Keep talking like that, and I'll give you a donation of my own," a thin, high-pitched voice complained from behind.

Relief coursing through his veins, Clint peered over his shoulder toward a slim man whose black T-shirt boasted a huge pair of scarlet lips. Must be the assistant.

Neil, his nose wrinkled as though he'd sniffed a particularly noxious odor, was fanning himself with a batch of papers. "Sorry to interrupt your charming conversation, but do you guys have your résumé and photo?"

Wesley smoothed his already sleek hair, rearranged his stance and handed over a glossy folder. "You need any first aid, just let me know. I'm a med student." He flexed his arms and positioned his hands on his hips.

"Gee, thanks. Remind me to check your bedside manner first." Neil froze in midswivel as his attention focused on Clint. His eyes widened as he digested Clint's appearance.

Heat crawled up Clint's neck. He bit back the explanation he'd been about to give that his banker's summons hadn't allowed him much time to freshen up. He resisted the temptation to fold his arms and hide the sweat stains beneath his arms. They'd have to take him as he was, or not at all.

Neil licked his lips and swallowed. "Your résumé and photo?"

"I, ah, don't have a résumé. Just a photo."

Gingerly, Neil plucked the strip of pictures from Clint's fingers, inspected the images, then turned the card over. "Name?"

The coffee in Clint's stomach soured. "What?" There was no way he could reveal his name in front of Wesley. It would jeopardize the past he'd buried.

"Since I'm not blessed with ESP, I'll need to mark your name, address and phone number on the back of your photo." Neil flicked his gaze over Clint, then raised a delicate brow. "Unless you have a business card?"

The offhand remark stung, increasing the discomfort that Neil's initial reaction had spurred. So what if

Clint didn't have a business card? Cattle didn't give a buffalo chip as to whether or not his name was inscribed on a piece of paper. What mattered was putting in a hard day of honest work at the ranch. Chest tightening, Clint straightened his shoulders, took a step forward and stared down into Neil's wide blue eyes. "Never needed one before now. That a problem?"

"Ah, n-no." Neil's glance sidled toward the next candidate. "No problem. Hey, everything's cool." He raised his hands in mock surrender before swiveling on his heel.

Stupid. The harsh studio lights glared accusingly. Closing his eyes, Clint dragged in a deep breath. Neil probably hadn't meant anything by it. And even if he had been trying to make a point, he was right in his implication—Clint didn't belong here. This wasn't Clint's world. It had been Kristin's, but never his.

Fragments of the events that had shattered his life swarmed him. Clenching his jaw, Clint banished the images. For nearly a decade, he'd kept his vow to never again allow this tainted industry to invade his—or Tia's—world. His gut twisted. What the hell was he doing here?

He should leave.

Now.

But his worn cowboy boots remained firmly planted on the gray concrete. He couldn't leave. It was his only chance to save all he'd worked for, to preserve his daughter's future. He would never let Tia down.

"Face the *back* wall, please."

The volume of Sonya's voice had risen a couple of notches and, instinctively, Clint knew she'd had to repeat herself for his sake. Turning toward its source, he peered down the line of preening bodies. A stand of lights blazed behind Sonya, rendering her hair a nimbus of gold, her body a slim silhouette with shapely legs.

Though she didn't know it, this unknown woman would single-handedly determine his destiny. After all his hard labor, the fate of the Silver S Ranch had come to...this. That in itself was failure. Shame writhed in his gut. Clint faced it, stared it down. Hell, he'd worn shame before. Failure too. Probably would again. What was important was not to let failure defeat you. And Clint Silver, aka Quicksilver, had never been a quitter.

He'd never felt more alive than he had at the starting gate, tension quivering his body as he strained forward, focusing on Olympic gold. Ready to pit his muscles and stamina against the design of the course, ready to adapt to the demands wrought by changing snow and weather conditions, and secure in the knowledge that he'd thoroughly analyzed his competitors in order to learn from their accomplishments as well as their mistakes. He'd painstakingly researched and obtained equipment that would allow him even the slightest technical advantage, and plotted the best possible strategy to gain that precious millisecond to put him ahead at the finish line....

Despite that he'd been carried away on a stretcher, he hadn't allowed that mountain to triumph over him. He'd gone back, more than a year later—without the television cameras to witness it—and had conquered its slopes. Granted, there'd been no time clock and he'd have never beaten it if there was, but he'd done it. Just as he'd always met every challenge head-on. Thrived on them.

Clint's adrenaline surged with the memories. To be a winner, he had to think like a winner. What was it Kristin had always said? The biggest sin was not to be noticed. So be it.

His pulse tattooing his temples, Clint swung around and focused his attention on the gray wall. He removed his hands from his pockets and straightened his shoulders, his head held high.

Like a prisoner awaiting the command of a firing squad, he felt totally exposed.

SONYA PAUSED BEHIND every man, minutely inspecting the merits of each backside, while Neil translated her visual response into written notes. Although all potential contenders had to be considered, she would not, could not, compromise by selecting an inferior specimen. She would far rather risk the consequences of her unfulfilled optimism than witness the mediocre results of a less-than-perfect butt.

"Major testosterone alert," Neil muttered in her ear.

Sonya looked up from a double-kegged bottom, shrink-wrapped in blue spandex, and quirked an eyebrow. This man had an overabundance of hormones, all right, but she'd bet Mother Nature had been assisted by more than a few synthetic supplements.

Neil shook his head, then inclined it toward the next prospect. Sonya turned, anticipating Neil's usual tactic of setting her up for some much-needed comic relief. But this time the joke was on her.

Shock slammed through her body, weakening her knees.

Before she could prevent it, a gasp slipped past her slack lips. The sound triggered a corresponding reaction, as muscles winked the denim that hugged the divine derriere.

Taut.

With a naughty little curve that invited lingering fingers.

Narrow hips melted into a tapered length of leg, all snugly sheathed in sun-bleached denim. A light blue shirt surged upward to encase granite shoulders that were only slightly softened by the sheafs of blond hair that straggled from beneath the brim of his Stetson, to brush his collar.

Raw and wild.

He was as out of place here as an unruly stallion among a herd of hogs, and just as magnificent. Lean. Windswept. He was solid simplicity, etched by the spare lines and curves of a master artist. Rugged and primeval. Potent.

Sonya moistened her dry lips with the tip of her tongue. Not her type, of course. She preferred polished, cultured men who knew which wines to order with each course of a gourmet dinner. This man looked as though a good meal meant a barbecued steak washed down with a beer or two.

A cowboy.

Not the type she wanted for this campaign. She needed someone more…refined. After all, the objective was to reach the high-end buyer, persuade him to spend his weekends in blue jeans. This guy looked like he'd arouse more impressionable women to dream about ripping the jeans off him, and totally forget their significant others. No. The cowboy's look was too…gritty. It was unfortunate.

Because he had a very sexy butt.

He had another strike against him: he was blond. She'd always envisioned the Rocky Ridge man as dark-haired and debonair, a James Bond type. Still, there was a certain magnetism—or was it tension?—about this guy. Uneasiness prickled her spine. Other than that he was a blond cowboy, what was it about him that set off alarm bells in her head?

His body language. He was so anchored to the spot, she doubted a bulldozer could have uprooted him. He'd be hell to work with. Like a high voltage wire emitted a pitched hum, he emanated high frequency defiance. She couldn't afford to risk her career on an unpredictable personality; he'd have to be eliminated.

Sonya itched to turn him around right then and there, to pinpoint a fault that would ensure his disqualification. But it wouldn't be fair to single him out at this point. She'd have to give him the same chance as the others, to determine whether he would be photogenic in still shots as well as video, plus give him a preliminary voice test. She'd process him, then dismiss him. After all, he was a cowboy, and if there was one breed of men she despised, it was cowboys.

Neil sidled in front of her as she moved toward the next candidate. "So?" he mouthed.

Her equanimity restored, Sonya shrugged.

Neil's eyebrows puckered, then relaxed as he tried to smother a smile. Using the clipboard as a shield, he tapped his fingers against his heart.

What on earth? Sonya frowned in confusion.

Writing rapidly, Neil angled the clipboard so she could read his note. "Pitter-patter?"

Neil knew darn well what she thought about cowboys. And why. Throwing her assistant an exasperated look, she motioned him back to business. She and the cowboy were from totally different worlds. And she intended to keep it that way.

Stepping around Neil, Sonya immediately discovered a surprise that could have saved her from her angst. Here was a candidate who almost exactly fit her mental image of the Rocky Ridge man.

Although this model was significantly smaller in stature than the cowboy, he was still of average height, and his limbs were beautifully proportioned. Granted, his butt was a little flatter, but he had raven-black hair and, most of all, an air of casual sophistication about him. Her search was half-over. Perhaps the best had been saved until last.

After a cursory survey of the remainder of the posing candidates, she strode to a vantage point from which she could view the entire lineup. She forced a deep breath into her lungs. "Please face front again."

As the group shuffled to face her, Sonya's expectant gaze zoomed in on the dark-haired man. He had the bone structure and demeanor of an aristocrat, and closely resembled a younger Pierce Brosnan. Perfect. Instinct told her this guy had experience; confidence radiated in waves from his relaxed stance.

A quick review of the remaining candidates confirmed their unsuitability. Except one. She couldn't oust the cowboy yet. His Stetson, assisted by the angle of the studio lights, cast a shadow across his features and obscured all but a square jaw and a pair of clamped lips.

Sonya consulted her clipboard and flipped through the photos. Surely this distorted photo-booth image was a joke. She expelled her breath in a controlled torrent. He must be a total novice. Was he hiding a chrome dome, or had he somehow discovered they were considering a cowboy image for the campaign and dressed accordingly, hoping to improve his chances? Regardless, his hat was the one barrier that prevented his immediate disqualification.

"Remove your hat, please." As soon as she heard her words, voiced harsher than she'd intended, Sonya instantly regretted her demand.

He didn't move.

Her trepidation grew as dead silence entombed the studio.

Obviously he didn't know who he was dealing with. "Excuse me, would you *please* take off your hat?"

The cowboy continued to defy her.

Conscious of the speculative stares riveted on both her and the renegade, Sonya knew she'd just succeeded in putting herself in a very awkward situation. Fatigue must be affecting her rationale. Now she was at a disadvantage.

Sonya's mind raced. How could she resolve this? With Harvey and Lawrence looking on, she couldn't back down; they'd perceive it as a lack of control. Somehow she had to defuse the situation, demonstrate the professionalism she'd built her reputation upon.

Then it hit her. This rebel was challenging her.

Why? And furthermore, should she answer his invitation? It wasn't the first time her authority had been tested and, no doubt, it wouldn't be the last. It was a fact of corporate life, especially when you were a woman. Under the same circumstances, Lawrence would expect any of her male associates to rise to the challenge. And so would she.

Sonya drew a deep breath, then moved.

Each measured step brought her closer to him. Still he betrayed no sign of yielding his hat. Committed to her course of action, she had no choice but to continue toward him. She contemplated the consequences of ripping the Stetson from his head, versus sweetly and patiently asking him to remove it.

Sonya claimed her territory in front of him, still unsure of her intended action. Licking her lips, she decided she'd try a reasonable approach. But before she could speak, he swept the hat off his head.

"Ma'am." He combed his fingers through honeyed layers of hair. "Meet your Rocky Ridge man."

2

STUNNED, Sonya stared into green-and-gold-flecked eyes that swallowed her into their depths. Fighting the unfamiliar sensation, she scrambled for the solid ground of reason. *Hazel.* She clung to the ordinary word as she gathered her deviant thoughts. His eyes were simply an unusual shade of hazel.

Long, sooty lashes and inky eyebrows clashed with his golden skin and honeyed hair, lending him a piratical appearance. Intrigued, Sonya explored further. The study in contrasts continued with ridged cheekbones sloping into valleys shadowed with faint black stubble. A lone laugh crease punctuated one tanned cheek, heightening his dangerous charm.

He was exactly what she'd imagined and wanted to avoid. The intensity smoldering within him indicated a wild streak. For years she'd witnessed, firsthand, the lewd and uncivilized behavior of drunken cowboys. The last thing she'd ever do would be to put herself in a position where she had to rely on one.

The cowboy's impudent grin mocked her. She narrowed her eyes. Was he really a novice, or a very seasoned professional? Someone who could have been...planted by Mr. Practical Jokester himself—Neil? A few months ago, he'd had them all hooting with laughter when, during a shoot, he'd tampered with the product for a cookie commercial. Sonya would never forget the look on the model's face when she'd pulled a blue oatmeal cookie from the brand name bag. Perhaps Neil was up to his old tricks.

Either that or the cowboy knew Neil. Because he was her confidant, as well as her assistant, Neil was aware of her cardinal rule and wouldn't dream of using his position to influence her decision regarding a friend of his. So this would be just Neil's style—to coach his friend on how to use dramatic effect to attract her attention.

Either theory made sense. This guy's timing was exemplary. He had to be a pro—an actor playing a "real" cowboy.

Now everything fell into place—Neil's alarm when he'd seen Lawrence and Harvey, the animated yet furtive exchange between Neil and the cowboy, and Neil's transparent eagerness to gauge her reaction. Wouldn't he have had a laugh if she'd admitted she found the cowboy attractive? Not that she had, of course. Sure, the man had a certain visual appeal, but certainly not an emotional one. Not for her, at any rate.

Until she discovered their objective, she'd play it by ear. She could give as good as she got, and she'd enjoy every moment of putting the dissident through his paces.

But first she'd answer his impertinent proclamation.

HAVING THROWN CAUTION to the wind, Clint held his breath as he witnessed Sonya's startled amber eyes narrow in speculation. Would his gamble pay off, or would she toss him out with a snap of her slim fingers?

She laughed, a clear, crystal peal. "Is that a fact? *You're* my Rocky Ridge man, are you?"

Desperate to keep up the charade he'd committed himself to, Clint winked. "Look no further, ma'am."

"Oh, but I'll have to take a closer look, a much closer look." She inched past the boundary of his personal comfort zone. "I have to ensure you possess all of the, ah, attributes I need."

As he breathed in her exotic scent, Clint's muscles shivered in response. Nerves, no doubt, or simply his proximity to the woman who held his future in the palm of her hand. A beautiful woman.

Like a crystal flute of champagne, Sonya was slim, delicate, elegant. Her burnished, pale blond hair barely brushed the shoulders of her biscuit-colored suit. Long, slim legs, encased in beige, fused into high heels the same color as her suit. His gaze returned to her eyes—eyes that gleamed like polished amber. The cool, confident and slightly contemptuous eyes of a woman in control. He was at her mercy. But he'd be damned if he let her see that.

"I've never had any complaints about my attributes before now." Knowing he had to brazen out his strategy, Clint rocked on his heels. Little did she know his attributes were in danger of atrophy from lack of use, although a remarkable recovery seemed to be in progress.

One of her arched eyebrows elevated. "Perhaps their standards weren't as high as mine."

"Well, you just haul out your yardstick and we'll see how I measure up." This was the old Clint who had claimed the top of the medals podium through sheer spunk and split-second instinct. Cocky. Living life on the edge.

A smile skulked along her lips. "Somehow, I doubt I'd need a stick that long."

"Ah, but you haven't seen the extent of my hidden qualities."

Sonya leaned closer, her eyes the intense gold of a mountain sunrise. "By the time I'm finished with you, cowboy, you won't have anything left to hide."

Her intimate whisper caressed his nerve endings and threatened to make his most hidden quality a source of attention. "Is that a promise?"

Contempt eradicated the glow in her eyes. "I don't believe in promises." Her ice-cold smile chilled Clint's heated blood. "But I always keep my word."

She swiveled on her heel and stomped back to her original vantage point.

"All right, gentlemen, you're free to go." Her voice was once again cool and brisk. "Except for you."

Clint's heart leaped as she pointed in his direction, then plummeted as she indicated Wesley.

That was it, then. The anticipation that had percolated in his veins was now as dark and bitter as the dregs of day-old coffee. He'd gambled and lost. Everything.

But it wasn't the things that mattered; mere things he could acquire again, eventually. It was the intangibles—Tia's heart-shaped face, wide-eyed with delight when a newborn calf had nuzzled her hand; the proud smile when she'd sat astride her first horse. With the ranch gone, they'd have to move to the city. Clint's shoulders sagged. There was no other choice. Even if he could hire himself out as a ranch hand, there was no place in a bunkhouse for a ten-year-old girl.

Silently, Clint cursed himself. Whatever he'd said,

it'd doused Sonya's interest like a thundershower liquefying dust to mud. Why had he egged her on like that, pretending to be something he wasn't? It never led to anything good. He should've remembered that.

"Oh, cowboy."

Instinctively, he responded, turning toward her before he registered her mocking tone.

"See you back here in an hour. And lose the hat, will you?"

Although her aloof attitude burned Clint like a rope chafing a bare palm, hope surged, drowning his self-recriminations. If he had to, he'd make a pact with the devil himself.

Or herself.

WHILE THE STUDIO EMPTIED, Sonya signaled for the high-powered lights to dim. No sense raising the electricity bill more than she had to. Almost instantly, the air cooled. The door to the control room opened, disgorging the tall and bulky Harvey Wilson and the even taller, but slender, Lawrence MacLeod. Sonya's head buzzed with fatigue as they meandered closer.

"Lawrence, this young lady of yours must've rode rodeo once." Harvey's barrel chest heaved with laughter. "She sure hog-tied that cowboy, but good."

"Harv, as you well know, I handpick our top executives." Lawrence's thin silver mustache rose with his smile. "It's their responsibility to ensure each project is completed as agreed, no matter what it takes."

Sonya hated it when people talked in front of her, without directly addressing her. She thrust her hand toward Wilson's wide palm, took a firm grasp and squeezed as she shook his hand. "Hello, Mr. Wilson."

"Now, little lady, I'm not going to tell you again—you call me Harvey. Mr. Wilson's my pappy."

Little lady? Sonya just managed to turn her wince into a weak smile. Surely he didn't mean to sound condescending; it must simply be his style. "Certainly, Harvey." She removed her hand from his crushing grip and flexed it before turning to her boss. "Good to see you again, Lawrence."

"Sonya."

His touch was cool and brief, as it always was now. A deep tan perfectly complemented his silver hair, piercing blue eyes and impeccable silver-gray suit. He wore his aura of privilege and wealth like a second skin. As she would, someday. "Been out on the golf course yet?"

"No, just arrived in town. Haven't even checked into my hotel." He turned to Harvey. "Did you manage to get us a tee-off time for tomorrow morning?"

"Six sharp." The larger man's eyes gleamed. "Not too early for you, is it?"

"Of course not. For some reason, jet lag improves my handicap." Lawrence's lean finger stroked the silver hairs symmetrically edging his thin upper lip. "I warn you, I'll be ruthless."

"Wouldn't expect anything else." Harvey eyed Sonya. "Care to join us, little lady?"

She knew if it had been left up to Lawrence, the invitation would never have been delivered; after all, she didn't belong in the old boys' network. Which was the precise reason she couldn't refuse the opportunity. Even though after today's exhausting events, the last thing she needed was a golf game at dawn. "I'd love to."

"Great. I'll pick you and Lawrence up at 5:30 a.m."

Harvey snapped his fingers. "Hey, maybe we can get the Rocky Ridge man to make up the foursome." He grinned at Sonya. "Though we'll still let you play from the ladies' tees."

"Thank you, Harvey." Sonya returned his smile. "I can't speak for the Rocky Ridge man, but as far as playing from the ladies' tees, it really isn't necessary." She directed her attention to Lawrence and looked him straight in the eyes. "I like to play on equal terms."

"Then play the ladies' tees. They were designed to give women a fighting chance." Lawrence's tone was as cool as his steely smile.

Harvey harrumphed. "So, little lady, have you found the perfect Rocky Ridge man?"

Grateful for the break in the tension, Sonya sought the warmth in Harvey's round face. "I think so. We have a few interesting prospects."

"That cowboy one of them? I kinda liked his style."

Sonya chose her words carefully. "Yes, everyone's a possibility at this point. But we have to run the candidates through a few critical tests before we choose the one who best exemplifies the qualities of the Rocky Ridge man."

"Good." Harvey brushed a hand over one jean-clad thigh. "Got a lot riding on these jeans." His face reddened as the implication of his words must have sunk in.

"We all have a lot riding on this campaign, don't we, Sonya?" Lawrence's voice was as smooth as polished mahogany.

She turned to face him. "Yes. And as such, I'm grateful to have been given the freedom to personally handpick my *own* team. Their individual and collective expertise will guarantee the success of this campaign." *Unlike the Saunders' account.*

Lawrence's steel-blue eyes locked onto hers. He hadn't missed the significance of her words.

"Are you giving me your personal guarantee?"

His lethal question sliced into the unhealed wound, scabbed with self-doubt. Sonya noted his avoidance of the word, *promise*. Lawrence knew better than to use it. Again. As her mentor, he'd been like the father she'd never known; and, like her father, he'd abandoned her. But she'd learned from her experience, learned to fashion her career, and her life, on her own terms.

Sonya lifted her chin. "Yes. You have my personal and *professional* guarantee." Her words sealed the deal. There wouldn't be any more chances if this campaign failed; her reputation would be shot and she'd be out of a job. However, if she succeeded, the anticipated revenues from this account alone should solidify her claim on the vice presidency. From there, she could write her own ticket, use her status to make the move to an international firm. She would prove herself. Not to them, but to herself.

First things first. She had to select her Rocky Ridge man.

"Fine. Harvey and I will indulge ourselves in some refreshments before you get under way again. Have someone notify us when you're ready." Without sparing her a second look, Lawrence steered Harvey out of the studio.

Neil, who was coming through the door, held it open and sent a mock salute after them as they swept past without a nod. Shaking his head, he crossed the empty studio toward her.

"So, how'd it go?" Neil handed her a cellophane-wrapped egg salad sandwich.

Sonya shrugged as she peeled off the plastic. "The usual. Harvey treated me with kid gloves, and Lawrence threw the glove down."

"That's his guilt showing through. There's something fishy about the Saunders' disaster. I saw your proposal and it was fantastic. There's no way they would have turned it down. Have you ever confronted him about it?"

"I tried to talk to him about it once, but he informed me potential vice presidents had to learn to roll with the punches."

"The bum. Oops." Neil giggled. "Am I getting fixated, or what?"

Her mouth full of dry bread and rubberized egg, Sonya rolled her eyes.

"Speaking of bums, which one are you going to choose for the Rocky Ridge man?"

Swallowing the cardboard food, Sonya stuffed her half-eaten triangle of sandwich back into its container. "Wesley has everything I've been looking for. A great derriere, good build, dark hair, terrific blue eyes, excellent facial structure and a masculine chest."

Neil snorted as he followed her toward her worktable. "He looks like a playboy."

She sighed. "Vintage James Bond. Women love that type—smooth, sophisticated."

"The love 'em and leave 'em type."

"Maybe she leaves him first."

Neil's eyebrows rose. "Like you always do?"

Sonya ignored him. "Why? Who would you suggest?"

In answer, Neil hummed "Home, home on the range."

"No way. The cowboy is too...earthy. When women fantasize, they want diamonds and champagne, not sweat and cow dung." Although she had to admit, the cowboy had demonstrated a quick wit during their recent verbal sparring match. She'd enjoyed their rapid repartee, but the cowboy had probably exhausted his supply.

"C'mon, sweetheart, don't kid yourself. Women don't want the calculating, civilized type with orchestrated moves, they want wild, unbridled passion."

Sonya tapped a tapered nail against the plastic sandwich container. "You've been watching too many Westerns, Neil. Besides, he doesn't have the right look."

"Then maybe we should reconsider the look. Think of it this way, sweetie. Men dream of being cowboys, women dream of having one."

"Not *all* women."

Neil acknowledged her sharp tone with a sheepish look. "Okay, the majority of women, then. We're talking mass appeal."

Neil's eagerness to champion the cowboy was a dead giveaway. All she had to figure out was whether he was setting her up for a practical joke or promoting his friend. "He's certainly dressed for the part, down to the scuffed cowboy boots and Stetson." She scrutinized Neil for a reaction.

A satisfied smile slid onto her colleague's face. "Mmm. *Mucho macho.*"

So Neil refused to admit the deception. In her books, that was tantamount to a challenge. It was payback time. The cowboy had put her on the spot earlier with that hat business. If he wanted attention, that's just what he would get. Anticipation raced up one side of her spine and down the other. She smiled. "That remains to be seen."

CLINT STOOD slightly apart from the other models, trying to forget that his daughter's future depended on him getting this job. Thank God the baby-sitter had been able to stay longer. Taking deep breaths, he forced himself to forget his own inexperience and, instead, appraise his competition. They all looked relaxed and confident. Unlike him.

"Cowboy."

His pulse hammering, Clint snatched his attention away from the nine candidates who'd also made it to the final selection process and focused on Sonya. "Yes, ma'am?"

She crooked her finger. "Would you come here? Please."

He noted that, despite her authoritative air, the harshness had vanished from her voice. She sounded almost friendly.

"Be my pleasure, ma'am." Clint ambled toward her, conscious of the daggerlike stares slicing into his back.

She pointed to a spot on the floor in front of a large, dark blue curtain. "Stand there and face the camera, please."

Clint obligingly turned and placed the toes of his boots against the strip of tape. Out of the corner of his eyes, he could see the speculative gazes of the other hopefuls.

"What's your name, cowboy?" Her tone was intimate, pitched low so the others couldn't overhear.

In an effort to moisten his dry throat, Clint swallowed. "Anything you want it to be."

Her golden eyes gleamed. "I see." She stepped closer to him, her arm almost brushing his.

Desire singed his nerve endings.

"Hmm, I guess I could call you Stetson, or..." her gaze swept his shirt "...Mr. Blue." Her eyes moved to his jeans, "or maybe Honey Buns." She stepped back, a small smile playing around her bronzed lips. "Which do you prefer?"

Clint's spine stiffened at her mocking tone. From the looks of her, Ms. Duncan had probably never experienced a real ranch. What he wouldn't give to see her tiptoeing around the cow patties in her high heels.

But he was on her turf now.

"I'd prefer to be called the Rocky Ridge man."

Sonya gestured toward the other candidates. "There're a few others who'd like to claim that title, too."

Clint's mind raced. If he revealed his name, the connection could be easily made between him and Kristin. Once the tragedy of the past poisoned the present, his chance to get the job and the cash he needed would be eliminated. Since he couldn't allow that to happen, he'd have to use a fake name. "Then call me Rocky."

"Rocky?" Her gaze traversed his body. "Actually, I prefer Rock."

He shrugged. "Fine with me."

A small smile played around her lips. "All right, Rock, let's see you strut your stuff."

This was it.

The final showdown.

But there was no way he could go first. He needed

time to do his homework. That's what training runs were for. Any skier who was in contention knew he had to watch his competitors, analyze their strengths and weaknesses, then apply the knowledge to his own performance.

Clint took a deep breath. "If you don't mind, ma'am, I'd like to let the others go first."

"And if I do mind?" Beneath the velvet timbre rang steel.

There would be no mercy if he were to admit any weakness. He forced an assured smile. "Just want to save the best for last."

"Ah." Sonya tilted her head and pursed her luscious lips. "Such confidence." She glanced over at Neil, then her eyes locked on Clint's. "Planning a memorable performance, I take it?"

He sure hoped so. "You bet."

Slowly, she nodded her head. "Okay, cowboy. Letting you perform last probably is the best idea. Less distraction for the others."

Although he wasn't quite sure what she meant, the small rush of victory boosted his battered composure. "Thanks, ma'am."

"Just one thing, cowboy."

Her quiet words lassoed his heart. "Yes?"

"Think twice before you mess with me. I don't take prisoners."

Confused, Clint nodded in acknowledgment. What on earth was she talking about? Feeling as skittish as a young bull in rut, Clint claimed his place at the end of the line.

Sonya beckoned to Wesley, spoke to him briefly, then turned to the rest of the group and waved them forward. "Please move in a little closer and watch

Wesley carefully. He'll demonstrate what I want the rest of you to do."

"First, look into the camera lens and state your name. Then turn and walk to the *X*." She pointed to the masking tape that marked the spot. "Stop, make a full turn, then walk back to this spot, look into the camera lens and read the lines on the TelePrompTer. Everyone gets one run-through, we tape the second. Got it?"

Wesley performed like a veteran show dog. Watching and listening intently, Clint noted Wesley's arrogant strut, his almost perfect diction and rhythmic inflections. Yet there seemed to be something missing from his presentation. A couple of candidates later, Clint realized what it was. Wesley had been too slick; he lacked sincerity.

Clint absorbed the best of each presentation, studied the television monitor for the facial expressions that worked and the speech patterns that best delivered the message.

All too soon, it was his turn.

"Rock. You're up."

Clint nodded and moved in front of the camera. Psyching himself up, he imagined himself at the starting gate of the ski course, staring at the ice-encrusted slope that dropped away from his skis. Adrenaline erupted, drowning all doubt.

"My name is Rock." He scowled at the rusty creak in his voice, cleared his throat and tried again. This time, he barked at the impersonal lens. Admonishing himself, he whirled around, stalked to the next mark on the floor, executed a sharp turn and strode back to his original position. Rattled, he tried to read from the

TelePrompTer, look into the lens and smile at the same time, but stumbled over the words.

He'd been too aggressive. Totally screwed it up.

Sonya sidled up to him. "Losing your nerve, cowboy?" Mock sympathy dripped from her words. "After all that boasting about your attributes, I was sure you would deliver a better *performance* than that."

A frisson of electricity leaped through him as her fingertip traced a pattern on his shirt. Desire slashed at Clint's heart; the desire to prove himself, the desire to win and...desire for her? No. Extremely bad idea.

He needed to concentrate on his one last chance. Staring at the floor, he clawed through old memories. There'd been that time when his agent had negotiated for a sports store endorsement. Anticipating an audition, Kristin had coached him on what to do. *Pretend the camera is your lover*, she'd advised. *Make love to it.* But after the Olympics, all deals had fallen through; corporations only wanted endorsements from winners.

Besides, there was no lover he could envision playing to. Other than a few mutually convenient liaisons, no one had piqued his libido in years. Except...

"Excuse me, ma'am, but would you mind standing closer to the camera?"

Her eyes narrowed. "Why?"

"It would help me, uh, focus a little better if I could talk to a real person."

Sonya shrugged. "I guess it's all or nothing for you now. You must have a gambler's heart, cowboy." With an economy of movement, she stood beside the camera, arms folded beneath the swell of her breasts. When her hardened nipples punctuated the silk, molten lust lanced through him, keener than it ever had.

He reached into the past, reclaiming the laconic charm of the young Clint Silver. Champion of the U.S. ski team, he'd been lauded for his talent, envied for his easy success with women, his confidence unblemished. He faced her now, the svelte blonde whose studied disinterest revealed her reluctance to acknowledge any attraction. The challenge was irresistible. He sent her a smile full of promise. "Hi, I'm Rock."

He turned and strolled away from her, conscious of her speculative stare following him. Nonchalantly, he turned and captured her gaze. Although caught out, she didn't falter, but boldly examined his firmly toned physique. His eyes locked on hers, he ambled toward her. Fire smoldered in the amber depths of her irises. Her bronzed lips pouted an invitation he didn't intend to refuse.

He halted. With his entire focus on her, he plucked the telescript from memory, savoring each phrase. "When a man wants the best, he demands the best." As he embraced her with his words, her arms unfurled, her hands finally resting on her thighs.

"And nothing but the best will do."

Her fingers flexed, drawing her skirt taut across her hips.

He slid his hands into the front pocket of his jeans, conscious of the pull of the denim across his groin. "Get the best…Rocky Ridge blue jeans."

Her heated gaze followed his hands.

He gave her an intimate smile. "Satisfaction… guaranteed."

In the utter silence that followed, Clint's trancelike state ebbed and reality leaked in. Sonya blinked, snatched her hands from her skirt and grabbed her nearby clipboard. Throats cleared and feet shuffled. Neil was beaming from ear to ear.

Clint swallowed hard; frissons of discomfort gyrated down his spine. What had come over him? He'd virtually exposed himself, like a wanton gigolo. What was worse, he'd enjoyed it.

Bile rose in his throat.

He was no better than a cheap hustler, and Sonya was nothing more than a purveyor of sex and illusions. Had he actually felt attracted to a woman who inhabited the same artificial world that Kristin had? That wasn't the kind of example he wanted to set for Tia.

Sonya tapped her clipboard with her pen, then clutched it to her chest like a shield. "Just one more thing, gentlemen. Since we're planning a shot where the Rocky Ridge man will be wearing only his jeans, I need to see your bare chest."

Her words arrested Clint. His luck had just run out.

The others immediately complied. Beside him, Wesley pulled off his polo shirt off to reveal a tanned torso, swathed with whorls of dark hair. Sonya inspected him, smiled approvingly and asked him to pivot in front of the camera.

Clint's heart thudded as she directed her attention to him.

"Rock?"

Noting the challenge in her eyes, he found all thought frozen, except for one thing. If he took off his shirt, Wesley would immediately know who he was. Clint had to avoid doing that, at any cost. Otherwise, the past would resurface, and Tia would be the one to suffer.

Then Sonya's fingers reached for his shirt. "Need some help, cowboy?"

Instinctively, Clint reacted, grabbing her arm. "What the hell do you think you're doing, lady?"

"Oooh." She pried his fingers from her wrist. "Spirited, aren't we?" Amusement glinted in her amber eyes. "Look, cowboy. I've put up with enough theatrics from you for one day." She ran a finger down the side of his face. "Cooperation goes a long way in this business. You want the job, you do what you're told." Her voice was an intimate purr. "If I tell you to drop your pants, you drop them. Modesty acts don't impress me. Skin sells in this business." She patted his cheek before stepping back and folding her arms. "It's your choice, Rock. Show me your chest or leave."

Disgust and anger consumed Clint. He wasn't some prize bull she could inspect for stud. He'd come here prepared to compromise, not to be compromised.

This was pure insanity. He needed to get out of here.

Without a word, he turned, lurched toward the studio door and bolted for freedom.

3

GOOD RIDDANCE.

Sonya welcomed the cowboy's abrupt departure. It was as if a heavy, scratchy sweater had been removed from her back, providing instant relief. And, oddly enough, a sense of loss. Like standing in a dark and deserted studio that only a short time before had vibrated with the exuberance and zest of the creative spirit, but now stood lifeless, a shell of a world scattered by abandoned props.

Good Lord, was she pathetic or what? The cowboy had been trouble from the start; she should be grateful he was gone. Temperamental talent only made everyone's job harder. And she still had work to do.

As Sonya's adrenaline level dwindled, her energy dissipated as fast as champagne bubbles. It seemed Rock had made her decision for her. Wesley would be the Rocky Ridge man. After all, he'd been very cooperative, and he matched the look she'd originally envisioned. Although it was too bad his pale blue eyes didn't possess the same intensity as the cowboy's.

Sonya looked at Wesley's smooth, smiling face. Why wasn't she experiencing that punch of certainty that always heralded a creative achievement? Maybe because the stuffing had been knocked out of her. This had been a most unusual and exhausting day.

She sighed and faced the nine models who remained. The lineup had dissolved into odd pairings and groups, abuzz with discussion. Only Wesley stood apart, still bare-chested, hands on his hips. It would be a pleasure to work with such a consummate professional, wouldn't it?

"Thank you, gentlemen. I really appreciate your patience and cooperation. We'll be notifying you shortly as to our decision. Wesley, could I speak to you for a moment?"

Slinging his shirt over his shoulder, Wesley swaggered toward her.

"Too bad the cowboy dropped out." He gave her a winning smile. "Obviously he's not cut out for this type of work. You need someone you can rely on."

His inference, and his nearness, left Sonya cold. Yet he was her first choice, wasn't he? She opened her mouth to offer him the contract, but no words emerged. Confusion fuzzed her brain. She needed some time to distance herself, to look at the situation objectively.

"Excuse me." Neil rushed up to Sonya and took her by the elbow. "Don't do it," he muttered in her ear. He raised his voice. "There's something I need to discuss with you, Ms. Duncan."

Ms. Duncan? This level of respect indicated something serious. She turned to Wesley. "Thank you, Wesley. I'll—"

Neil tugged her away.

"—call you."

"I'll be waiting." Smugness oozed from his voice.

Sonya glared at Neil. "Yes, *Mr. Barclay*, what is it?"

Excitement glowed in Neil's face. "Forget the pitter-patter scale, sweetie." His voice tickled Sonya's ear. "We're definitely talking the Richter scale."

Sonya kneaded her forehead with her fingers. "What? Who?"

Neil sighed gustily. "Later. Here comes the big brass and the big brash." He squeezed her arm. "Trust me on this. Don't make any decision until we play back the videotape."

"Well, well." Lawrence slipped a slim electronic notebook out of a suit coat pocket and entered a notation. "Looks like you owe me fifty, Harv." He snapped the case shut and put it back in his pocket.

Harvey scowled as he removed a thick billfold from his back pocket. "Hold on now, let's double-check before we jump to any conclusions."

Lawrence raised an elegant silver brow at Sonya. "I do believe, just as I predicted, Sonya has had the good sense to select the more, uh, civilized candidate for the job. Isn't that right, Sonya?"

The foul taste in her mouth was due to more than endless cups of instant coffee and a few bites of a plastic sandwich. *They'd bet on the models, like horses?* Sonya swallowed her distaste and managed a weak smile. "We're very close to a decision. So close, in fact, I want to reserve final judgment until I have a chance to review the tapes of the session."

"Oh? I rather approved of the choice that was made for you." Lawrence's feral smile belied his bored tone. "Surely you aren't leaning toward prairie primitive?"

"Now, see here, Lawrence," Harvey blustered. "I don't want a namby-pamby in short white pants selling my jeans. I want a damned cowboy who looks like he knows the meaning of work!"

"Gentlemen, gentlemen." Neil clapped his hands. "Let's be careful of being too subjective. Perhaps we should allow the lady to do her job." He smirked at Sonya.

If she hadn't been so thankful for Neil's interruption, she'd have reminded him just how subjective his own earlier choice of "Mr. Liquid Eyes" had been.

"That's right. My money's on the little lady to pick the right man for the job."

"I think part of the problem is that both Rock and Wesley are striking men, and that either one could be the Rocky Ridge man." Sonya chose her words carefully as she guided them toward common ground. "We need to refocus on the advertising strategy and determine which man can best assist us in reaching the goals we've set for the campaign." She herself could certainly use the reminder.

"Yep. This gal knows her stuff." Harvey nodded his head at Lawrence. "Bet she could even teach old dogs like us a few new tricks, eh?"

"Who do you think taught her everything she knows?"

It was a sobering thought. Lawrence had taken her under his wing when he'd been vice president of marketing and she'd been a junior art director. He'd guided her through the shoals of the shark-infested corporate sea, requesting nothing but her loyalty. And she'd learned to swim with the predators, earning her credentials the old-fashioned way, through hard work.

Yet, since the Saunders' fiasco, Sonya had discovered minuscule cracks in Lawrence's smooth veneer. Enough to give her pause. But at this point, when she was so close to achieving her first major career goal, it was hardly the time to shed her mentor. Especially when he'd given her so much.

"What say we leave this to the young 'uns and go rest our weary bones?" Harvey slapped his arm around Lawrence's shoulder. "I'm ready for a slab of barbecued beef and a quart of the best whiskey you can afford."

"So, you're waiving your right to approve Zenith Communications' final selection?"

"Hell, no. I'm just saying I know your little lady will pick the right man for the job."

Lawrence pulled out his electronic notebook. "You willing to put any money on that?"

"Double my fifty."

"You mean mine."

The two men laughed.

"Just leave a message if you decide to skip the morning golf game." Lawrence tossed the words over his shoulder at Sonya as he and Harvey took their departure.

GOOSEFLESH PRICKLED Sonya's arms as Rock's provocative video image filled the living area of her hotel suite, repeating his vow of "satisfaction...guaranteed." Yes, he was rough, but he breathed life into the script, made it vibrate with an emotional edge. The magic enveloped her once again and desire lanced through her, as keen as it had a couple of hours ago, when he'd looked her in the eyes and uttered the words. The combination of nonchalant charm and restrained intensity had been impossible to ignore. It had taken all her willpower not to dissolve into a puddle at his feet.

No one had ever evoked such wanton sensations, and she'd believed no one ever could. So she'd fought the exotic elixir that had sedated her mind and aroused her desire. Spurred by denial, she'd found contempt to be her only defense, and she'd attacked him with an uncharacteristic vigor, until she'd driven him away.

What was it about him that generated such... passion in her? The foreign feeling scared her now, as it had then.

"Any significant damage?" Neil cast her a sidelong glance as he aimed the remote control device at the VCR and rewound the videotape.

Sonya doodled on a corner of her notepaper. "From what?"

"The major seismic activity on the tape." Neil shifted in his armchair and, positioning his elbow on its arm, propped his chin on his hand. "Want me to run Wesley's performance again?"

She sighed. "No. You were right. Compared to Rock, Wesley is as flat as tepid ginger ale." She crossed out Wesley's name. "Thanks."

Neil's gaze was sympathetic. "I know it was difficult for you, since cowboys aren't exactly your favourite breed of man."

Few people knew the sordid details of her childhood. It had taken the disillusionment of a failed relationship, and a bottle of chardonnay, before she'd sobbed the details onto Neil's shoulder a couple of years ago. "I guess I did allow it to prejudice my judgment. A little." She smiled. "But you never let up on me."

"I knew you'd recognize his latent sensuality, once you'd allowed yourself to."

"It won't be a smooth ride. I have a feeling Rock and I won't see eye to eye on anything."

Neil grinned. "Ain't that the truth."

"But we'll make this work, won't we?"

"It'll be worth the effort. He'll be fabulous."

"Okay. We'll trust our instincts and take a chance on him." Sonya pushed the clipboard toward Neil. "Since I don't have any coordinates for him, I'm sure you won't mind giving Rock a call. See if you can set up a lunch meeting with him tomorrow."

Neil's eyes widened. "I—I can't!"

"Really, Neil." Sonya blew out an impatient breath. "Well, if you have a problem with it, give me his number and I'll call him."

"I don't have it." Neil's fingers clawed at his hair, loosening long strands from his trim ponytail. "He took offense when I asked him for it...." His voice trailed off. He turned to Sonya. "I'm sorry."

Panic spasmed in Sonya's throat. "I don't get it. Isn't he a friend of yours?"

"No. I don't have the faintest idea who he is."

THE COOL TWILIGHT AIR raked Clint's hair as the pickup truck consumed the blacktop highway in front of him. There was a new whine in the engine he hadn't heard until now.

Dammit all to hell! He punched the horn, holding it down and letting it blare across the empty landscape until his frustration drained away. He'd come so close, then reality, and Sonya Duncan, had checked him but good. The thought of easy money had blinded him to the possibility he could be identified. From what the newspaper ad had said, he'd thought they'd just want a few photographs of someone wearing blue jeans. Preferably a back view.

He hadn't counted on television being part of the deal. Even if Zenith had offered him the contract, how could he possibly have accepted it? Recognition would resurrect the scandal and initiate a media feeding frenzy. Seven years ago, the media had feasted on dissecting the demise of a superstar. The sleazy tabloids had been the worst. And now there were the tabloid-style TV shows; they'd all knock themselves out to dig up and reveal every dirty detail of the glamour, sex and drugs.

This time Tia would be old enough to understand, old enough to be devastated. His first duty was to protect her from the truth about her mother. He might lose the legacy he'd tried to build for his daughter, but he'd preserve her innocence if it cost him his last breath.

What had made him think he could enter that artificial realm and remain untouched? Just look at the way he'd responded to Sonya. How could he possibly be attracted to a woman like her—a woman who peddled sex to the masses? The thought stung.

Sliding behind the purplish foothills in the distance, the setting sun stained the clouds with intense variations of red, orange and pink. It would be a fine day tomorrow and, hopefully, on Sunday, too.

He'd try to make this final weekend at the ranch a special one, so he'd wait until Monday to tell Tia the news. Unless a miracle happened by next Friday, the bank would foreclose on the property. The manager had said they'd give him a couple of weeks to relocate, but Clint knew he wouldn't be able to stay on the land, knowing it was no longer his.

He'd stop in at Kowlawski's store and make sure he bought a lottery ticket for tomorrow night's draw. He swiped at his face with a hand. More pipe dreams.

Well, it had been a farfetched idea in the first place.

Ten or twelve years ago, he'd have been able to carry it off; but the Clint of his youth was long gone, matured by life and its circumstances. As a single father, he had responsibilities to uphold. Responsibilities he'd sworn to seven years ago, when he'd cuddled a somber three-year-old in his arms and looked past her strawberry curls to the white-and-gold coffin suspended above the freshly dug grave. He would never allow Tia to be exposed to the despair and degradation that had claimed her mother.

SONYA STARED at her assistant, who clutched clumps of his frazzled hair. "Tell me this is one of your sick jokes, Neil."

"I wish I could."

"Good God."

"What are we going to do?"

She massaged her temples. "We finally find our Rocky Ridge man, he disappears and we have no way to contact him."

"I'm really sorry."

"It's not your fault, Neil. I was the one who scared him away." Sonya got up, walked to the VCR, ejected the tape and enclosed it in its sturdy case.

Neil finger-combed his hair and pulled it back into a tidy ponytail again. "Something still doesn't make sense to me."

"What? The fact I'm such an ogre that men run away from me?"

"Now that's a switch." Neil's quick grin faded. "No, Rock seemed so determined to win—I saw him studying all the candidates when they did their auditions. So why would he suddenly take off like that?"

Returning to the sofa, Sonya placed the cassette on the coffee table. "Especially after he'd made good and sure he had my undivided attention." She shook her head. "Neil, I have a confession to make. I thought he was an actor you had planted, until he flubbed his run-through." Sonya rubbed a finger over her bottom lip. "I could tell by the panic on his face that wasn't supposed to happen. And I almost felt sorry for him, until…"

"Until he penetrated the force field that is supposed to deflect even your most persistent suitors?"

"He did not!"

"Sweetie, your eyes positively glazed over. Mine would have, too, if he'd turned his sensual spotlight on me."

"Nee-ill!"

"Okay, okay. So, where do we go from here, boss lady?"

"Neil, you're a genius!"

"I am?"

"That's exactly what we're going to do—spotlight him."

"Could you, uh, translate that for me?"

Sonya grabbed her clipboard and flipped to a clean sheet of paper. "Get me that publicist we talked to last week, get ahold of someone, anyone, at every local and provincial newspaper, and order a carafe of coffee from room service."

"Sure. What's up?"

"We're going to find Rock."

EARLY MONDAY MORNING, Clint leaned against a fence post and watched the day gently unfold, a bitter fatalism warring with the denial that refused to succumb to reason and die a quick death. He was about to lose more than his property and possessions, more than the stable sense of community that sprang from the common purpose and challenges he shared with his hard-working neighbors. He was going to lose a part of himself.

He faced the towering wall of stalwart mountains as they shed their dark cloak of night. They were ever changing, yet permanent. Clint envied their durability, their somnolent power, as immovable as the bureaucratic policies that could usurp the tangible bond between a man and his land.

Yes, the bank could confiscate his property, but they couldn't destroy his love for it.

Even now the essence and vitality of the earth enveloped him, thrumming through him as it nurtured and energized his spirit. To his left, a field of wheat shivered, whispering hope in the rosy light of dawn. The unfettered joy of birds greeting the sunrise roused his regret as he drank in the cool, pure air. He closed his eyes, determined to store every poignant detail in his memory.

When the heat of the sun had sponged up the cool air, he made his way back to the ranch house.

"Hi, Dad." Tia pointed to the machine at the end of the counter. "I made coffee." Her deep blue eyes shone with accomplishment. "Since you treated Katie and me to a weekend camping trip in the foothills, I'm cooking breakfast this morning."

"Great, sweetheart." Clint poured a cup into his favorite chipped mug. "Thanks. Anything I can do to help?"

"Nope, I got it all under control."

The enticing smell of sizzling bacon tantalized his

nostrils as he sat at the table in the middle of the sunny kitchen and drank deeply of the pungent, dark brew. "Tia." He waited until she turned, then saluted her with the mug. "You make a fine cup of java." He ignored the egg foam that dripped from the lip of the bowl Tia cradled in the crook of her arm.

"Oh, Dad. You always say that." A radiant smile lit her face as she returned to her task of whisking eggs.

A spurt of pride shot through Clint. At least he'd done one thing right. Although it had been as frustrating as hell at times, he'd learned to work with Tia's fierce streak of independence, teaching her the basics of self-sufficiency both in the house and on the ranch.

As his daughter set the bowl down and reached for a skillet, her slim arms struggling with the weight of the heavy cast iron, Clint refrained from offering his help. He also resisted the urge to reach out to the tumble of red-gold curls that swayed across her thin back. A few years ago, he could've yanked a tendril, then played innocent when Tia accused him of the deed. She'd end up pouting half-seriously and he'd send her into a fit of giggles with playful kisses and hugs.

However, she was a preteen and getting too old for all that now. His little girl was growing up, and she was looking more and more like her mother. Her thinness was transforming to slenderness; her budding beauty was blossoming. Clint's fingers tightened around his mug. Tia wouldn't follow in her mother's footsteps. He'd make sure of that.

A clover-laden breeze nudged the calico curtains, parting them with its impudence, allowing a bright sunbeam to dart inside and forge a golden path across the honeyed wood of the table. Absently, Clint rubbed the patina, finding comfort in its familiarity. Despite that most of their furniture would have to be sold, the table would go with them. It was their touchstone, the one consistent place where they joined with one another, a testament to family—him and his daughter.

How could he explain to a ten-year-old that he'd failed at the basic task of keeping a roof over her head? Sure, he could give her the list of excuses that had led him deeper into debt: unexpected natural disasters that induced artificially inflated feed costs, and a declining consumer demand for beef that resulted in prices so low he'd lost money over the past three years. Then he could try and explain his final gamble to meet an increasing demand for organically fed beef by mortgaging their ranch to the hilt in order to purchase top-quality breeding stock. He'd almost made it. Just a few more months and he'd have been able to get a premium price on his herd, make a dent in repaying his debt. But he'd run out of money. And time.

Now he had to pick the best time to tell Tia about losing the ranch. If he told her now, it might spoil her whole day; and with only a couple of days left, he wanted her to enjoy the carefree bliss of youth. Yet shouldn't he tell her now, so she could get mentally prepared for the move to the stifling confines of a city apartment? Allow her time to say proper goodbyes to her friends?

Clint dug his fingers into his hair. He was a no-good, sniveling coward. He dragged in a deep breath. "Tia, there's something I—"

The phone shrilled, delaying the inevitable.

"I'll get it." Tia set the butter knife aside and turned

down the heat under the skillet before grabbing the receiver. "Silver S Ranch." She paused. "Hi, Katie."

As Clint rose to gather the plates and cutlery for breakfast, a squeal from Tia stopped him in his tracks.

"Dad! Katie's horse is foaling. Right now. Can I go and help? Please?"

Tia's face glowed with excitement. She and Katie had been following the mare's pregnancy with all the anticipation of first-time midwives. "Sure, go ahead."

"Thanks, Dad!" She conferred briefly with Katie, then hung up the phone. "Breakfast's ready." Grabbing two slices of toast, Tia quickly assembled a scrambled egg and bacon sandwich. "I'll eat it while I saddle Zork." She plucked her Stetson from its peg near the back door, then rushed over to give him a kiss on the cheek. "The newspaper's there." She pointed to the antique pine buffet. "I'll call you once everything's over. Bye."

Clint dumped the remaining eggs, bacon and toast onto his plate, refilled his mug, then ambled back to the table. With Tia gone, the oppressive silence of the kitchen threatened to overwhelm him. Only a couple of days more and they'd both be gone. Futility flooded through him.

In an attempt to chase his blues away, Clint switched on the radio. A soft country ballad swelled forth, detailing the woes of lost love. "Great," Clint muttered. "Misery loves company." He speared a chunk of bacon and chewed it slowly. Although he didn't have much of an appetite, he wasn't going to let good food go to waste. Before long, food might be a tad more scarce.

"Rock, where are you?" a soft female voice crooned.

Clint sputtered his coffee all over the front of his shirt. Ignoring the sticky warmth, he stared at the speaker on the radio. He couldn't be more surprised if Sonya Duncan had materialized in the room beside him.

"This morning, I'm here with a beautiful lady who's in search of a man. But not just any man...." The rich baritone voice introduced Sonya and her agency. "Tell me a little more about this guy," the invisible announcer urged.

"We've invested a lot of time and money in our search for the right man to represent Rocky Ridge blue jeans, and late Friday afternoon, we found him." Sonya sketched the background details. "So, we need to talk to Rock."

They wanted him? Clint tried to control the hope that gushed through him.

"Then why didn't you just call and offer him the job?"

"Due to extenuating circumstances, we weren't able to locate him. But we're confident a program as popular as yours will reach Rock."

"Thank you, Ms. Duncan." The announcer's voice became more intimate. "I'd do just about anything to help such a lovely damsel in distress obtain her heart's desire."

There was a slight pause. "Yes. Thank you." Sonya's voice regained its sense of purpose. "On behalf of my client, I'd like to express our appreciation of your assistance in this matter."

"But you aren't taking any chances, are you? I understand you're running advertisements on all the radio stations and in all the newspapers in Alberta."

"Correct. It's imperative that I find him."

"We'll be in touch with you for updates. Anything you want to say to Rock?"

"Yes. Rock, we're prepared to make you a generous offer. Please call me at my office. We need you, cowboy."

Stunned, Clint sat still, gradually becoming aware of the cold coffee stains that plastered his shirt to his chest. Was this a dream born of his desperation? Had he imagined the whole thing?

He strode to the buffet, seized the morning paper and whipped through the pages until he came to a full-page ad. *Rock, where are you? Rocky Ridge blue jeans needs you.* The words were huge, taking up half the page. Thank God they hadn't used one of his awful Polaroid photos—probably because he'd looked more like a desperado on the run from civilization than a model. The remainder of the text echoed what Sonya had said in her interview. Her name and business phone number were at the bottom of the page.

They wanted him.

They were prepared to make him a generous offer.

Shock, surprise and relief chased each other up and down his spine. He might not lose the ranch, after all. He let out a whoop of joy and threw the paper into the air. Moments later, scrambling through the scattered newsprint, with shaking hands, he reclaimed the ad. Clint stared at the telephone number at the bottom of the page, then glanced at his watch. It was seven-fifty. He'd have to wait until Sonya reached her office. He'd call at eight-thirty. No, he shouldn't appear too eager; he'd wait a few hours.

Ripping off his wet shirt, he reached for a tea towel to wipe the dampness from his skin. The cloth slid over the gnarled and puckered scar that ran from beneath his rib cage to his hip. Reality seeped in as the coffee stains rubbed off. Shards of doubt ripped at his optimism.

He wasn't a model. He didn't have the talent or experience to carry this off. After all, his final audition had been a total fluke; chances were, he could never repeat it.

Besides, how could he possibly step forward now? With all the hype Sonya had created, the media would slather over him like a ravenous dog. He wouldn't be able to avoid revealing his identity or prevent the reporters from digging into his background. The repercussions would destroy the stability and values he'd instilled in Tia. And she'd learn the ugly truth about her mother—a truth he'd concealed, not by direct lies, but through avoidance. His daughter would suffer for the sins her mother had committed.

He wouldn't allow that to happen.

As usual, he was stuck between a rock and a hard place. Unless...

The germ of an idea began sprouting in his mind. Maybe there was a way....

4

HER NERVES SCREAMING, Sonya stared at the ringing phone. All morning it had been ringing, nonstop. Punching the intercom, she raised the receiver to her ear. "Is it another reporter, Annette?"

"No. Another Rock."

Sonya sighed. Her public relations strategy was a success. Maybe too much so. Every mainstream and fringe media outlet in southern Alberta wanted to interview her. And she'd complied; it was the one way she could reach the man she knew only as Rock. What she didn't enjoy was having to deal with the dozens of calls from kooks who claimed to be Rock.

She needed the man she'd unceremoniously tossed out of the audition. She needed to get his signature on a contract. Immediately.

"How does he sound?"

"He didn't make any lewd suggestions or practice any heavy breathing. In fact, he has one sexy voice. Line six." Annette hung up.

It was him. Anticipation shimmied down Sonya's spine. A sixth sense told her it was Rock. She took a deep breath and punched line six. "Sonya Duncan."

"Grapevine has it that you want to talk to me."

At the sound of his husky rumble, gooseflesh prickled the skin on Sonya's arms. "Rock," she breathed.

"Yes, ma'am. The one and only."

"Not quite." Relief washed through her. It *was* him.
"What?"

"Never mind, it's not important." Sonya moistened her dry lips and tried to project her usual professional tone. "I'm glad you called."

"I heard you on the radio. You said you wanted me."

Her pulse pounded in her eardrum, held tight against the phone. She swallowed. "No, I said *we* wanted you. Zenith Communications, Rocky Ridge blue jeans."

She was met with silence, deep and black. Sonya's throat constricted. Why had she corrected him? She couldn't take a chance of offending him! What would she do if he hung up? Just as she opened her mouth to speak, Rock cleared his throat.

"Of course, I didn't mean you...personally." His voice sounded stiff.

Damn. "I'm sorry, I didn't mean—"

"Look, what's this all about? Interviews on the radio, ads in the newspaper. Do you want me or not?"

Sonya gripped the phone tighter. "Yes. We're interested in talking about you becoming the Rocky Ridge man. But I want to present the offer to you in person."

"Okay. When and where?"

Had there been a tinge of relief beneath the cockiness in his voice? "Are you free for dinner tonight?"

"Can be."

Lawrence had taught her that when you're negotiating tricky deals, it was best to keep your opponent off balance; then, when you made them an offer, they were less likely to quibble over the terms. Rock would be on her turf at an upscale restaurant. And if all else failed, she'd have Neil there with her. Maybe they could do a variation of the good cop, bad cop routine. "I'll make reservations for eight o'clock at the Panorama, the revolving restaurant at the top of the Calgary Tower."

"No. Not there."

His brusque tone stymied her. "Why not?"

"I have my reasons."

Any other man who'd just been told he'd been selected for a plum assignment like the Rocky Ridge contract would be falling all over himself to accommodate her. But not the cowboy. Really, she'd have been much more comfortable dealing with a civilized man like Wesley. "What reasons?"

"*Private* reasons."

She was about to press the point, but bit her lip instead. "Where, then? No doubt you know the city better than I do."

"The Steak 'n Stein." He recited the address. "Meet you there at seven."

"Okay." She'd get there first and establish a position of power. "If we get there ahead of you, we'll grab a table." She snapped her elongated pen back into its holder.

"We?"

"Neil and I."

"No." Rock's tone brooked no argument.

"Excuse me?"

"Come alone."

A prickle of uneasiness ran down her spine. "Why?"

"Because that's the way I want it."

Sonya's ire rose. "You're pretty sure of yourself, aren't you?"

His low chuckle rumbled through her. "I figure

anyone who went to the amount of trouble that you did to lasso my attention must have some powerful need."

Dammit. Every time she thought she'd managed to get one step forward, he forced her two steps back. "And since you took the time to call, I trust it's a mutual need," she retorted.

"Mutual need," he murmured. Silence swelled, for one heartbeat, two. "Sometimes need can be a dangerous companion."

His words unnerved Sonya. For all she knew, this man could be a dangerous commodity, to her and to Zenith Communications. Could she allow the success of the Rocky Ridge campaign, and her future career, to hinge on the hope he would take direction from her? "Listen, is there a number where I can reach you, in case I need to reschedule?"

"No. If you don't show, I'll call you at your office tomorrow morning at 7:30 sharp."

The line clicked in her ear and Sonya grimaced as she hung up the phone. She'd pegged him, all right; he was a steak and beer man. A somewhat unfamiliar breed, yet she had the distinct feeling her unease was based on more than the simple fact he was a cowboy. His evasiveness had heightened her innate misgivings about him. After all, he wouldn't even give her his phone number.

Maybe she could confide her doubts about Rock to Lawrence, in private. Together they could sway Harvey, convince him they needed someone they could rely on, someone they'd worked with before. Or maybe they could test-market both Wesley and Rock, before taking the campaign public. It would take more time and money, but it could be worth it in the long run. The whole campaign centered around the Rocky Ridge man. If things didn't work out with Rock, it would be impossible to change models midstream. And impossible to salvage the vice presidency.

The phone rang again. "Yes?"

"Mr. MacLeod's on his way in to see you."

"Please hold my calls, Annette."

Sonya grabbed a tissue and blotted the perspiration that, despite the air-conditioning, had collected on her upper lip. She'd barely finished when the door to her office was flung open and Lawrence strode past her desk. With all the grandeur of royalty, he folded himself into a leather easy chair and signaled for her to join him.

"Lawrence, what a surprise." She rose, crossed to the informal meeting space and lowered herself onto the edge of the matching sofa.

He propped his fingers beneath his sculpted chin, a severe look on his face. "I had a call from Harvey. Seems his phone has been ringing off the hook. Reporters, television cameras, the works."

Sonya squared her shoulders. "I'm sorry if they've harassed him, although I did warn him that this publicity would spawn intense media interest. I'll call him and apologize for his inconvenience."

"Relax, Sonya. He's not complaining. In fact, he's ecstatic." Lawrence crossed one knife-pleated trouser leg over the other. "Sales are up in every store."

"That's wonderful." Sonya forced a smile, but knew it was devoid of sincerity. Why had Lawrence toyed with her like that? "I'd anticipated the publicity would raise awareness of the Rocky Ridge name. It's all part of the strategy." Thank God her risk had not only paid off, but was working much better than she'd anticipated.

Lawrence frowned. "I must tell you, I think this is a high-risk strategy you've chosen, Sonya. You've created high expectations with the client that you may not be able to live up to, let alone surpass. There are so many variables at play here that I wish you'd discussed it with me first. If it fails, you're going to fall flat on your face." He studied his well-manicured hands. "I won't allow Zenith Communications to share the blame for your...independent decision. My secretary is drafting a memorandum to that effect."

Sonya's blood chilled. He was isolating her; there'd be no company net to land in if she needed one. "And if I succeed?"

A smile slivered Lawrence's face. "Then, of course, it's business as usual."

"Either way, Zenith wins."

"Naturally."

Sonya nodded. "And your *impeccable* reputation is preserved."

Lawrence lifted a silver brow in acknowledgment. "Anyone can climb the corporate ladder, but only a genius stays at the top." He pulled a slim cigarette from a silver case, tapped one end against it, then inserted it into a short silver stem. "Found the cowboy yet?"

"Just got off the phone with him. I'm meeting him tonight."

"Another questionable judgment. The man's an amateur, an unknown factor. But Harvey's insistent we sign him." Lawrence snapped his matching silver lighter shut and released a controlled stream of light blue smoke. "Guess you have your work cut out for you, don't you?"

She couldn't appeal to Lawrence for help. Not now. Besides, she'd committed herself to a course of action when she'd initiated the media search for Rock. It would take all her skill and ingenuity, plus her team's focused efforts, to maintain the momentum of this campaign. Sonya slid her sweaty palms into the pockets of her suit jacket. "I'll manage."

Lawrence flicked ashes in the general direction of the ashtray. "Odds are stacked against you."

"And the vice presidency?"

"Pull this off and it'll be within your reach."

"That's not good enough."

Lawrence's eyes narrowed. "Oh?"

"If I succeed, I want you to guarantee me the position."

"Playing hardball, are we?"

Sonya met his gaze. There was no going back now. Lawrence nodded. "Deal."

"I want it in writing."

Lawrence's lips compressed. "I'll have my secretary forward a letter to you. And I want a progress report tomorrow morning." He shrugged. "I stopped believing in miracles a long time ago."

"I don't intend to fail."

"Good." Lawrence stood and strolled past her. Harsh tobacco smoke wafted over her. "Failure is not an option."

CLINT NOTICED SONYA as soon as she stepped through the door. She stood out like a nursery-bred rose in a field of scrub. Her red dress skimmed her body, flirting with the curves beneath, yet blatantly revealing her long legs—a contradiction like the lady herself. Damn, she was one fine-looking woman. But off-limits.

Because he wanted to ensure she was alone, Clint sat back and watched as Sonya removed her sunglasses, then tucked them into a pocket of the black briefcase that dangled from a strap on her shoulder. She rearranged the matching suit jacket that was folded over her arm and peered at her watch. As her eyes no doubt adjusted to the darkened interior of the restaurant, she began a visual search of the nearby tables. When a large-boned cowboy returned her cursory glance with a clothes-melting stare, Clint stood and strode toward the door.

Time for his Rock persona. He'd better make it damn good, because when he laid out his conditions for accepting the contract, there was a mighty good chance she'd give him his walking papers. But it was a risk he'd have to take.

When she saw him, the frown that furrowed Sonya's forehead disappeared and her rosy lips curved in greeting.

"Rock." She held out her hand.

"Sonya." His hand engulfed hers.

Her grip was firm, her touch cool. For a moment, they stood appraising each other. Clint held himself rigid as Sonya's gaze swept down from his white shirt and black bolero tie to his black denims, to his ebony cowboy boots. He quashed the resentment that reared within him; he didn't know if he'd ever get used to being inspected like some prize bull. One thing for sure, he'd never be able to look at a cattle auction in the same light again. "Hey, I even washed behind my ears. Honest."

"I'll take your word for it." Sonya radiated confidence, her amber eyes clear and direct, all-business. "I'm glad you called."

"How could I resist such a heartfelt request?" He'd need all the charm he could muster to get past her brisk attitude and establish a personal rapport, since his whole strategy depended upon determining whether he could trust her. Clint gave her the slow smile that, years ago, had warmed the heart of many a snow bunny. "I'm impressed."

"Oh?" She raised an elegant brow.

"I've never had a woman go to such lengths to line up a dinner date with me."

She shrugged. "Then I must warn you not to feel too flattered. I often conduct business over dinner. After all, the Rocky Ridge contract is of mutual interest to both of us."

"Right, that's, uh, what I meant." Yep, he had his work cut out for him. Clint pointed toward the back of the restaurant. "I have a booth waiting."

He led her past denim-clad couples on the dance floor, whose frantic movements caused their fringes to whirl and their rhinestones to glitter while their cowboy boots thundered against the wooden floor. Sonya gave the dancers a wide berth, as if afraid an errant boot might crush her red-tipped toes, encased in fragile sandals.

She claimed one side of the wooden booth and Clint folded himself into the other. A server in a denim miniskirt and white, embroidered blouse materialized and plunked a glass of ice water in front of each of them. Setting down a couple of vinyl-bound menus, she asked for their drink order.

"You want a beer?"

Although he couldn't hear Sonya above the music and stomping, Clint deciphered the words by reading her lips. He shook his head. "I'll have a vermouth, on the rocks."

Sonya blinked, but made no comment, and consulted with the server herself. When the girl left, she frowned and leaned forward. "I can't hear myself think, much less talk," she shouted. She glared at the gaudy jukebox that squatted at the edge of the dance floor, as if her censure might silence the rowdy tune that wailed above the clatter of steak knives and the thud of beer steins on thick-topped wooden tables.

Clint gestured at the dancers, then at the barn board walls that sported antique leather, wood and metal implements. "Not your usual style, huh?"

Her nose wrinkled. "Reminds me of the barns I once toured at an historical settlement."

Clint would've preferred the quiet elegance of the Panorama himself, but since it had been Kristin's favorite restaurant, the maître d' would have most likely recognized him. He'd only been to this restaurant a couple of times with friends, and figured it would have the kind of atmosphere that discouraged eavesdropping. Plus it had the added advantage of a rear exit to the parking lot.

Sonya pointed to an acne-pocked youth in a checked shirt and blue jeans, who sat astride a machine that tossed him up and down. While he held on for dear life, a group of his friends cheered him on with catcalls and whistles. "What's that?"

"A mechanical bull."

"A what?"

While her attention was diverted, Clint moved around the table and slid onto the polished wooden bench beside Sonya. His thigh kissed her leg, clad in sheer hose.

"There, now, isn't this better?" His voice purred in her ear, stirring her hair against her neck. He breathed in her fragrance, the scent reminding him of rambling roses nodding along the fence in sun-warmed fields. Not at all what he'd expected from such a sophisticated businesswoman.

Sonya scrunched herself into the corner of the booth, putting a few inches of open space between them. She grabbed her menu and held it up in front of her, like a shield. "I'm left-handed. So unless you want to battle over elbow space…"

"That's a mighty tempting proposition." Clint stretched his arm along the back of the booth and scrutinized her. "But I usually wrestle my women in bed, not on a restaurant table."

"Save it for the cameras, cowboy." Sonya set her menu down and folded her arms. "Let's get one thing straight—I'm here to discuss the Rocky Ridge blue jeans contract. What about you?"

Dammit, she'd sidestepped him as neatly as a contrary calf at branding time. Perfect. For his plan to work, he needed to be able to trust her, to ensure she'd keep his secret. "I think it's time we got to know ea—"

Movement at the restaurant door caught Clint's eye. Like ravenous dogs, a petite brunette holding a microphone and a man with a television camera balanced on his shoulder clawed their way through the crowd on the dance floor.

"*Damn!*" Clint jammed his black Stetson on his head and grabbed his battered leather jacket as he flung himself out of the booth. She'd betrayed him. "I should have expected it from someone like you!"

The image of Sonya's startled amber eyes burned in his mind as he slammed his hand against the metal bar of the back door and launched himself through the exit.

SONYA THREW a twenty dollar bill on the table and scrambled out of the booth, almost plowing into the cameraman and reporter that Rock had been so eager to avoid. They shoved a camera lens and microphone into her face.

"Was that the mysterious Rock?" The reporter's blue eyes gleamed with excitement.

"No, that was my cousin. He's camera-shy." Until she had a signed contract, the identity of the Rocky Ridge man had to be protected, just in case things didn't work out with Rock.

"Really." The reporter's sharp eyes searched Sonya's face. "Have you heard from Rock yet?"

Although Sonya herself had stimulated the media interest, it was in Zenith Communications' best interest for her to manage it. She waved the question aside. "As soon as we have something to announce, I'll be calling a press conference. Gotta catch up to my cousin." She sprinted after the cowboy, cursing her strappy sandals; she hadn't bargained on a foot race. But the cowboy wasn't going to pull his disappearing act on her again.

Bursting into the evening light, she fumbled for her sunglasses and thrust them on. Rock was wrenching open the door of a nearby, dilapidated pickup. Sonya raced to the vehicle, clutched the handle of the passenger door and flung it open as the truck sputtered to life. "I need to know why you took off like that."

"What the hell—" Rock glared at her from under the brim of his hat as he gunned the engine.

"Either you have great instincts or you're running scared of the media. Which was it?"

"Back off, lady. I don't have time for this right now."

"You'd damn well better make time. I'm on a tight schedule myself." She threw her briefcase and jacket inside and thrust herself upward, one foot gaining purchase on the floor of the truck while her hand grasped the edge of the plaid seat. Her skirt hitched higher as she propelled herself into the cab. Rock's eyes flicked to her exposed thighs. The heat in his gaze ignited her determination. "We're going to settle this contract tonight. Or else."

"Or else what?" Rock snarled.

"Or else I'll find another guy who wants to be the Rocky Ridge man."

The camera crew burst through the restaurant door. Rock swatted the heel of his hand against the clutch.

Sonya barely had time to shut the door before the truck careened out of the parking lot and sent her sprawling against the cowboy. Her left elbow landed against an iron-hard thigh, only inches from his groin. Heat rising in her cheeks, Sonya scrambled to the far side of the cab and secured the seat belt around her. "What the hell is your problem?"

"You said you'd come alone." His words were as sharp as splintered glass.

"I did."

"Then who were those two in the restaurant? Clark Kent and Lois Lane?"

Sonya sighed. Nurturing talent had never been her forte, and the cowboy's lack of industry experience meant she'd probably have to assign him a baby-sitter. "Reporters looking for an update on the Rocky Ridge story." Office buildings lurched by in a blur. "Look, is there somewhere we can stop and discuss this rationally?"

"There's a park nearby."

"You'll have to get used to it, you know."

"To what?" Suspicion tinged his voice.

"The publicity. You're well on your way to becoming a celebrity. I know it can be overwhelming when you're not used to it, so I'll see that you get some coaching on media relations."

Rock remained silent, his knuckles white against the steering wheel.

"Of course, it all helps to sell blue jeans, and I must say, it's a great start to the campaign." God, why was she babbling so much? Giving him excess information could be dangerous; he might use it as leverage to up his fee.

Keeping his eyes on the road, Rock nodded, then cleared his throat. "Why didn't you use my photo in the newspaper ad?"

Glad that he seemed prepared to discuss business, Sonya shrugged. "They weren't exactly the most flattering shots." She sent him an apologetic smile. "First impressions count in this business. For maximum impact, our art department has designed a fantastic campaign to properly introduce the Rocky Ridge man."

Abruptly, Rock stepped on the brakes and turned

into a park snuggled against the Bow River. The air shimmered gold from the descending sun. Couples cuddled and families strolled, while children and dogs frolicked along the walking path.

Rock shut off the engine and turned to face Sonya. He stretched his arm along the back of the seat. Beneath the civil veneer of white cloth, his chest and arm muscles flexed with a primitive power. "I have a confession to make."

"Oh?" His masculinity surrounded her with its palpable presence. No man had ever made such a physical impact on her like this. And she'd be damned if she'd allow a fickle cowboy to be the first one. She fought the heat that threatened to liquefy her resolve. Where was her usual control? After all, she'd learned a bitter lesson about mixing business and personal relationships. "What is it?"

Rock swallowed. "Reporters make me nervous."

"No kidding." *Great.* A publicity-shy model-cum-spokesperson was exactly what she didn't need to contend with. "Why?"

Rock busied himself unbuttoning a cuff and rolling up a sleeve of his shirt. His tanned forearm was dusted with golden hairs. "Us cowboys don't generally attract much notice from the media."

"You will as the Rocky Ridge man."

Rock paused in his task of rolling up his second sleeve. "So, your offer's still open?"

"I wouldn't be here if it wasn't. The question is, are you interested?"

Giving his sleeve a final twist, Rock nodded.

"Good." She snapped open her briefcase and drew out two copies of the proposed contract. "Why don't you look this over?"

He thumbed through the pages, then set it against the steering wheel. "Just give me the highlights. I'll have my lawyer review it in detail, later."

Sonya leaned over, turned to the last page and pointed to a figure. As her hand grazed his bare arm, the shock of awareness zapped the oxygen from her lungs. She drew a steadying breath and sat back. "That's how much we're offering."

A silent whistle streamed from his lips. His hand rasped over his chin. "All that for speaking a few lines in front of a camera?"

"Not quite. We start with still shots for billboard, magazine and newspaper ads, then we'll graduate to radio and television ads." She flipped through her own copy of the contract. "As you'll note on page four, initially we're retaining your services for two months, with an option to renew for up to another year."

"Can you strike the renewal clause?"

Smart move. If things went well, he'd be able to negotiate a higher price later. "Will do." Sonya smiled in relief. "Why don't you take it home, review it and call me tomorrow?"

"There's a condition or two I need to add."

Sonya's heart sank. Of course it couldn't be that easy. "Conditions?"

"I, uh, have a pretty bad scar." Rock pointed to his left side. "I don't want it to show."

Ah. So he wasn't immune to vanity. That's why he hadn't wanted to doff his shirt at the audition. Funny, his concern seemed at odds with the overall casual demeanor he'd displayed to date. She nodded. "I'll make sure it won't. Our makeup artists can accomplish miracles with latex and body cosmetics. Anything else?"

"I want to keep my weekends free."

He must have a girlfriend. Why did disappointment thunder through her at the thought? Sonya nodded. "That's already taken care of. I like to maintain a regular work schedule and avoid overtime. That way I can make sure my team isn't stressed out. Is that it?"

"Just one more thing."

His terms were reasonable so far. A lot of professional models had pages of the specific brands of food or beverages they would require. Rock definitely didn't seem like the Perrier or vegetarian type. Maybe he wanted Fred Flintsone-size portions of ribs for lunch each day. "What's that?"

Rock averted his face and stared out the windshield. "You can't reveal my identity...."

Sonya frowned. "I suppose we could give you a pseudonym—"

"No. You don't understand." He turned toward her, his eyes an intense green. "You can't show my face."

5

SONYA'S FROWN MELTED like lard in a cast-iron pot. For a few seconds, Clint witnessed the effects of blank astonishment before her jaw actually dropped and her amber-colored eyes widened. He wondered if there was a hope in hell of him getting the contract.

She blinked, then a tentative smile broke over her face. "You're kidding me, right?"

Holding her gaze, and his breath, Clint shook his head. "Nope."

Confusion clouded her eyes and stitched tiny lines around her mouth. "Let me get this straight. You expect me to use you as the Rocky Ridge model and spokesperson, but I can't show your *face?*"

He had to convince her to hire him, without revealing the secrets from his past. In his experience, the advertising industry had no conscience and embraced tragedy as a valuable commodity that drew intense public interest. Kristin herself had used the publicity surrounding his parents' death and his Olympic accident to stimulate media coverage, in order to enhance her own public profile. He couldn't take a chance that Sonya might exploit Kristin's death for the same reason. Clint wouldn't allow the truth about her mother to shatter Tia's innocence. By concealing his face, he'd protect his daughter. Clint stuck to his resolve. "That's right. You can't show my face."

"Why not?"

"I can't tell you."

She grimaced. "Somehow I get the feeling we've had this conversation before." Pivoting, she faced the dashboard and stared out the windshield toward the fiery horizon.

The gentle light softened Sonya's pristine profile and haloed the gold of her hair with fire. Her skin, bathed in the last blush of the sunset, looked as delicate as rose petals. Clint squelched a sudden urge to stroke her face, to stoke the sensuality she kept cloaked beneath her business facade. Beautiful women had only ever brought him trouble, and with a few words, this one could change his life. For better or for worse.

Sweat prickled Clint's underarms. He turned, cranked his window down and gulped the scented evening air. The faint hope he'd cherished began to fade, as did the dimming rays of the sun. When he swung back, Sonya's face was firm with determination.

"Are you in trouble with the law?"

Sordid memories squirmed like a pitful of snakes. Clint clamped the lid on the poisonous thoughts and shook his head. "The only thing the police want from me is an invitation to my end-of-summer barbecue."

Relief erased the sternness of her expression. "We're so close to finalizing this deal, I don't want to lose it."

"Neither do I."

"Good." Her lush mouth curved in a brief smile.

An uncontrollable urge to kiss her lips seized Clint, unexpected in its intensity. Given the imposed intimacy of the truck cab, and the fact he hadn't been this close to a desirable woman in months, it was understandable. But not wise. Clint settled back in his seat, leaned against the driver's door and draped an arm over the steering wheel. "So, where do we go from here?"

Sonya tucked her hair behind her ears. "Let's identify what we both need from this deal, then maybe we can work out the details."

She looked to him for confirmation, so he nodded.

"I need you to convey a message from my client, Rocky Ridge blue jeans, to its potential customers—" her slender fingers wove through the air "—urban professional males who nurture a secret dream to be a cowboy. We think you have the ability to deliver that message, but you'll have to take direction from us so we can deliver results to the client. Understood?"

Clint nodded, admiring the earnestness that animated Sonya's face and eyes as she spoke. Her gaze, golden and incandescent, seeped into him, eroding the hard edge of his distrust, replacing it with the hard edge of desire. And igniting feelings long dormant. For a brief moment, he indulged himself, savoring the sensuality he'd denied for so long.

"So, what do you need?"

Her question caught him off guard. He almost replied, "You." Instead, he reined in his rampaging emotions and, to gain some time, parried her request. "Now, that's an open-ended question."

"Level with me, cowboy. I don't have time for games."

Playing games had never been his style. It was Kristin who had excelled at playing games, both professionally and personally. Games that had decayed her morals, and their love. He'd never had any use for games. But wasn't that what this whole modeling gambit was about? Posturing and pretending until the pretense became reality, like it had for Kristin? The thought sickened him.

Yet the alternative frightened him. He'd lose the ranch and, forced to live in a big city, his daughter would be exposed to all kinds of materialistic influences. No, he had to go through with this. He'd just have to walk a fine line, projecting the self-confidence and sex appeal demanded of him, without succumbing to the seduction of living the lie.

The only thing that could help him now was the truth. First, he had to determine whether he could trust her. "Before I tell you what I need, I want you to give me an honest answer to a question."

Sonya quirked an eyebrow. "I don't give any other kind of answers."

"Why did you choose me as the Rocky Ridge man?"

She worried her lip. "Well, you have a certain, uh, raw talent. And…" She snapped her lips together and directed her attention to her briefcase.

"And?"

Her finger skated back and forth over the gold clasp before she looked up and met his gaze. "The owner of Rocky Ridge blue jeans preferred you." Defiance sparked in the amber depths of her eyes.

"But you didn't."

The air thickened between them.

"No." Her chin hitched higher. "Look, this campaign will make or break my career. If I succeed, I'll be vice president of Zenith Communications. And, I'll admit, it would be preferable to work with an experienced professional."

"Which I'm not."

"You're certainly...unpredictable."

"You know nothing about me." He hadn't meant for his words to come out sounding like a challenge.

"Exactly." Her eyes narrowed. "That's the problem. You keep running out on me, you've withheld your address and phone number from me, and now you're trying to hide your identity." She shook her head. "Why did you even audition in the first place?"

"From what the ad said, I thought you'd only want to snap a few pictures of my...my..." He ran a finger around the inside of his shirt collar, trying to find an inoffensive word. "My...hind quarters."

Her lips twitched. "Such a delicate way of phrasing it."

So the lady did have a sense of humor. The thought warmed him, produced a corresponding smile. "Maybe I've been around animals too long." He shrugged. "But that's what I do for a living."

She sobered in a flash. "Right. You're a cowboy."

"Not quite. I'm a rancher."

"So, why does a rancher want to model blue jeans?"

It was time for the truth. Or at least as much of it as he had to reveal.

Sonya watched the muscles of Rock's lean face contract. His reticence appealed to her. In a business where emotional outbursts often flowed as freely as incessant cups of stale coffee, it was a refreshing change. But if this oh-so-charming cowboy didn't open up to her, there would be little hope of working out a contract with him. The only way to resolve their impasse was to get to the root of his problem and find a solution. Fast. She pasted what she hoped was an encouraging expression on her face.

"If I don't get this contract, the bank forecloses on me."

His quiet statement thundered with unspoken emotion. Sonya reeled under the burden of responsibility that the knowledge instantly shifted onto her shoulders. Now she understood why he'd been so tense during the audition, why she'd detected such desperation within him. Losing your home was traumatic. As a child, she'd experienced the helplessness of moving from neighborhood to neighborhood, losing friends, changing schools. As sympathy for Rock threatened to swamp her professional perspective, she struggled to cling to the anchor of reason. "So, unless I hire you, you'll lose your ranch?"

"My home, my animals, my equipment..." His voice roughened. "Everything I've worked for."

Rock's eyes were bleak, and Sonya sensed the anger in his voice was self-directed. So he had as much riding on this deal as she did. "All the more reason for us to come to agreeable terms."

As he leaned forward, the cowboy's masculinity surged around her.

"I have to be able to *live* with those terms." His jade-green eyes glowed with intensity.

Sonya fought the force of desire that swept through her traitorous body. Why couldn't she control her response to this man? Not only was it unwanted, it was unacceptable. She held herself rigid. "So do I."

He acknowledged her words with a slight tip of his head.

She had to tread carefully, to make sure he didn't clam up again. She moistened her dry lips with the tip of her tongue. "And, as far as I can tell, there's only one condition preventing us from cementing this deal."

"The fact you can't show my face."

"It's really quite an unreasonable request."

"I can't sign the deal unless you include it."

"And I can't sign it if I do."

His gaze met hers, head-on.

Stalemate. What were her options now? Lawrence's last words echoed. *Failure isn't an option.* Her stomach tightened. After her show of bravado with her mentor, how could she return and admit defeat in closing this deal? Somehow, she had to alleviate Rock's fears and convince him to trust her.

"Look, if you're worried about unwanted media attention, I can assign a public relations person to keep things under control."

"A baby-sitter?" A wry smile curved his lips. "Thanks, I appreciate your offer, but you don't understand." He sighed. "It isn't a matter of controlling the media. I have to avoid them altogether."

This was the crux of the matter. Would he confide in her? Sonya's fingernails bit into her palms. "Why?"

"I can't let them know who I am."

"Why not?" Trepidation trilled down her spine. "Oh, my God. You're in a witness protection program."

"No, it's not that." Rock sat back and scoured his chin with a weather-roughened hand.

Sonya chafed at the raspy sound. His reluctance to confide in her indicated a deep struggle. Maybe he needed a little prodding. "You told me you're not in trouble with the law, so why on earth do you need to hide from the public?"

He dropped his hand, as if resigned to his fate, and stared at her, his eyes an intense green. The gathering dusk crept into the hollows of his face, accentuating the vulnerability etched there. "Otherwise, someone I love very much could get hurt."

His tender tone evaporated her impatience and tore at a susceptible corner of her heart. What astonished her, even more than the depth of passion in his voice, was her sudden envy of the person who elicited such ardor. Hadn't Sonya learned, firsthand, the consequences of uncontrolled passion? Unlike her mother, she would never allow herself to be crippled by her emotions. No. She'd learned to follow her head, not her heart, and she had a job to do here. "I don't understand. How could your modeling blue jeans possibly result in someone else getting hurt?"

Rock's features hardened. "That's as much as I can tell you. I'll be placing her at risk if I say any more."

So, he was willing to sacrifice his ranch for this woman; how typical of the weakness spawned by love, that it made people dependant upon others for their happiness. Luckily, she'd found fulfilment in her work, and she'd do her best to concentrate on the reason she was here—to sign up the perfect Rocky Ridge man.

But the more she heard, the less she was convinced Rock was the man for the job. She lifted her chin. "And I'd be placing my client's campaign at risk if I agreed to hire someone whose face I can't show."

"I see."

"I'd hoped we could somehow work around your demand, but you're asking me to put myself in an impossible position." Sonya turned and fumbled for the door handle. "I'd be insane to negotiate a contract under these terms. Not even Harvey would disagree with me on this one."

"Funny, I wouldn't have pegged you for a coward."

Like a lasso, his words curled around her. Shock scalding her senses, Sonya whipped around to face him. Rock lounged in his seat, his arms folded in judgment. She punched two words past the outrage that clogged her throat. "Excuse me?"

"Do you always leave when the going gets tough? I would have thought a Zenith Communications executive would have more grit than that."

That did it. All her pent-up frustration, her conflicting thoughts as to Rock's suitability and her fear of being wrong either way, exploded. "Luckily, my expectations of you were much lower. You're just as down and dirty as I would expect a cowboy to be."

Rock leaned forward, wedging her between her seat and the truck door. "And you're as ornery as a wild mare that's been cornered in a corral. Instead of dodging the bridle, you'd do better to take the bit and run with it."

"How dare you compare me to a...a barnyard animal!" She raised her hands to his chest and tried to shove him back, but beneath his shirt his warm, solid chest was immovable. His heat, his scent, his sheer physicality licked at her nerve endings, causing tremors of awareness to roll throughout her body.

"Honey, believe me, there's nothing like you in my barnyard." His teeth flashed white in the gloom. "Thank God."

The amusement in his voice infuriated her, as did her unwanted response. She lifted her chin in defiance and raised her eyes to his. "And your point is?"

"Sonya, you're missing my point altogether." His voice gentled. "In order for us both to win in this situation, we have to work together. Agreed?" He moved closer, his gaze locked on hers, until their mouths were only a whisper apart. His warm male musk, mingled with a faint aroma of sunlit forests, enveloped her.

His potent sensuality unnerved her. If she didn't do something quickly, Rock would kiss her. Her searching fingers grasped and pulled the door handle, and she ducked out the door.

Taking deep gulps of air, she reached in for her briefcase. Rock was halfway out his own door, but he wouldn't stop her. She'd walk to the nearest pay phone and call a cab. But when she turned, he stood inches away, trapping her between him and the truck.

"I didn't mean to scare you off." He stepped even closer, his eyes intense, his voice low. Intimate.

Desire thrummed in the air between them. She had to deny the insanity. Sonya lifted her chin, stared into his eyes and fought a drowning sensation. "I'm not scared of you."

She was scared of herself, of her reaction to this man. The thrill of danger imprisoned her in its grip. She'd never experienced such raw power, never sampled such intoxicating magic. Until now.

Her breath caught in her throat.

Then Rock's mouth claimed hers.

Firm, yet gentle, his lips promised passion, tempered with tenderness. Heat furled from the contact point, unleashing devastating waves of sensation that threatened to dissolve the remnants of her defenses. He drew her to the brink of a foreign realm where intimacy tangled with vulnerability.

It terrified her. No man had ever exposed this intimate world to her—a realm that would exact a price guaranteed to induce the loss of self, leading to the self-destruction her mother had experienced.

Besides, did this cowboy think he could dissolve her resolve with a touch of his lips, that she'd allow a business decision to be influenced by this...bone-melting...kiss? No! Her mother's weakness wouldn't become her own. Sonya fought against the languorous heat that liquefied her muscles.

Retreat was the only possible option. But she was trapped.

In Rock's arms.

KISSING SONYA was like falling, inch by wonderful inch, into a meadow of sweet-smelling wildflowers. Her heated breath fed Clint's desire and her softness molded against his hardness. He savored her taste, her texture—until she pushed him, hard.

Thrown by the force of her shove, he took a step back in an effort to regain his balance, but tripped on a rock. Instinctively, his arms tightened around Sonya as he stumbled backward in an awkward dance. But the impetus of their combined weight defeated gravity, and he slammed onto the ground.

Clint opened his eyes to find Sonya lying on top of him. Light spilled from the interior of the truck, onto the hard-packed dirt that edged the parking lot. He groaned, his shoulder and back aching from the impact of their tumble. "I guess that's what they call an earth-moving kiss."

"Next time you want to move earth, I suggest you romance a backhoe." Sonya wriggled as she tried to free herself from his arms, her actions only serving to stimulate his already aroused manhood.

With her face flushed, either from her realization of his desire, or from her own exertions, Sonya struggled to upright herself. In the process, her elbow bit deep into his ribs. Clint drew in a sharp breath. "Ouch!"

Her golden eyes gleamed. "Lust hurts."

"I think it's love."

"Well, I think it was a mistake."

"Then I hope you'll accept my apology." He held her gaze. "But I was referring to the saying, 'Love hurts.'"

"Love, lust, what's the difference?" Sonya stood and crossed her arms. "Other women might enjoy your fancy lip work. But it doesn't influence me. Or my decisions." She brushed at the dirt clinging to her dress.

Just like she was brushing off their soul-stirring kiss. If he were smart, he'd ignore the memory of her body tight against his, the primal craving that still surged through him. The kiss, which had been initiated by a spark of curiosity, had accelerated into an uncontrollable wildfire that had threatened to consume them both. Why had he allowed impulse to override his better judgment?

Clint watched as Sonya picked up her fallen briefcase and purse, setting them on the seat of the truck. She was all-business, as usual. So why was he mooning over a simple kiss, like a pathetic adolescent? He should consider himself lucky that she seemed willing to forget it, that she might not use the kiss as an excuse to get rid of him, once and for all.

Or was she simply denying her own response? He

was certain that, just before the impact of hitting the ground had separated their fused lips, she'd not only succumbed to his hunger, she'd displayed her own appetite.

Pushing himself up to a sitting position, Clint reached beneath his leg and retrieved one of Sonya's sandals. His best bet would be to follow her lead, to pretend nothing had happened. But first he wanted to confirm his suspicion about her reaction. Standing, he handed Sonya her sandal. "Tell me how you managed that."

Her head snapped up, her eyes meeting his. "What?"

"How you made sure you got the soft landing."

"Trade secrets." She gave him a self-satisfied grin. "Besides, I'd hardly describe your body as…soft."

"Oh, how would you describe it?"

She looked down at her hands and vigorously wiped them together. "Perfect for the Rocky Ridge advertising campaign. That is, it would have been if we had reached an agreement on the terms."

"You know where I stand."

Sonya sighed and nodded in resignation. "If it was just a photographic campaign, we could probably have worked around it. But with television commercials…" She shook her head.

"For someone who's been put in charge of such an important campaign, I would have expected you to have more confidence in your abilities."

His words had the desired effect.

Sonya gasped, her face paling. She planted her hands on her hips. "How dare you! You know nothing about my creative abilities!"

"Not true." Tucking his thumbs into his belt, Clint

leaned back against the truck. "On the contrary, I personally know you can be quite brilliant in your media strategy."

"How on earth..." Sonya's wrinkled brow cleared. "Ahh. The 'Rock, where are you?' campaign."

"Exactly."

"But that was different—it was a one-shot deal. I knew if the mass media grabbed the idea, somehow, somewhere, you'd hear about it."

"And it worked."

Sonya folded her arms under her chest. "Yes, it did."

Inspiration struck. Maybe he could turn this situation to his advantage, after all—by convincing her to turn the one-shot deal into a continuing series. "Why? Tell me what was it that made the media grab it. Why did those reporters follow you to the restaurant?"

"Curiosity. We piqued the public's insatiable thirst to obtain the answer to an otherwise unanswerable question. Now they want to know who the Rocky Ridge man is. There's no magic to that."

"That's where you're wrong."

"Get to the point, cowboy."

It seemed she called him cowboy when she wanted to assert her authority, or when she was on the defensive. From the little he knew about the industry, she'd no doubt had to fight her way up to have risen to such a position of prominence within Zenith Communications. That suggested she was no stranger to adversity. "Why are you still here?"

Sonya blinked. "Because I'm, uh..." She chewed on her lip. "I'm...I still think there might be a chance of rescuing this deal."

"Uh-uh. I already told you, in no uncertain terms, that I won't change my mind. So why haven't you left?"

"You tell me, cowboy."

"It's the mystery. You couldn't leave without knowing why I wouldn't show my face."

"But you did, finally, tell me."

Clint nodded. "So why didn't you leave then? Because I aroused—"

Sonya's eyes narrowed to glittering slits. "Don't flatter yourself, cowboy," she interrupted.

"—your curiosity. You're still here because you want to know the rest of the story. Right?"

"Does that mean you're going to tell me?"

"No."

Sonya picked up her purse and looped the strap over her shoulder. "I don't see where this is getting us."

"You're not into mysteries, are you?"

"I'm just about fed up with this one."

"Okay, okay. I'm a confirmed fan myself, and there's nothing that drives me crazier than not being able to solve a good mystery."

"So?"

He played his trump card. "So, don't let the public solve this one."

"You mean, keep the Rocky Ridge man's identity a secret?" Sonya laced her fingers together, staring into midair before addressing him again. "It's an interesting idea. But it would mean redesigning the entire campaign."

Clint pushed away from the truck. "Of course, it would take someone with exceptional skills to pull it off...."

"Someone just like me…and you?"

He concentrated all his sincerity into his eyes. "I'll do whatever it takes."

"There's more than just you to consider here."

"Look, I know it's a risky situation for you."

"You don't know the half of it."

"It's been my experience that there comes a time when you can't play it safe, when, in order to win, you have to be prepared to lose it all."

"Like your ranch."

"And your career." Although he'd personally survived that catastrophe, he'd witnessed the helpless horror of Kristin's inability to cope with her loss of self-identity. He'd never want to see anyone else experience the same devastation. He'd make it his personal responsibility to ensure Sonya would never be placed in that situation. All he had to do was to have faith in himself, again. To regain his old competitive confidence. Clint squared his shoulders. "Believe me, if it works, the rewards will exceed your greatest expectations."

"*If* it works."

"Bottom line—" Clint tapped his derriere "—the end justifies the means."

A mischievous look crossed Sonya's face. "In this case, I'd say both our ends are on the line."

"It's a bum rap."

Sonya laughed, a peal of pure silver. "You and Neil would get along great." Her smile erased the strain on her face, replacing it with a warmth that tugged at something in the vicinity of where Clint's heart had once been.

"Then it's a deal?"

6

SONYA KNEW THIS WOULD be either the best or the worst decision she would ever make in her career. There would be no in-between. Rock's suggestion had power in it, magic. It also had great potential for failure.

Zenith Communications always preferred a more conservative approach, but what would be the best for Rocky Ridge blue jeans? The publicity generated by her search for Rock had produced extraordinary blue jeans sales already. If they quickly and carefully built on the initial exposure, they could accelerate the public's interest. Pulling it off would be an advertising coup. Rocky Ridge would dominate the blue jeans market. And the vice presidency of Zenith Communications would be hers.

Anticipation trilled through her at the thought. On the downside, if they failed, her career would hit rock bottom. But if she played it safe, she'd never know whether she could have done it or not. It all hinged on faith, in herself and Rock. Could they pull it off? She'd provide the grit and determination, he'd supply sheer audacity, and they'd both have to hope Lady Luck joined the team. Sonya met his gaze. "Yes. We have a deal."

His eyes remained steady on hers. "You won't regret it, I promise."

Now that she'd committed to a final decision, Sonya's resolve consolidated. "I don't intend to."

"Good."

"Because one false step and we're history."

"ROUGH NIGHT?" Neil plunked a mug of steaming coffee down on Sonya's desk the following morning.

"Mmm?" Sonya punched a revised figure into her spreadsheet program and clicked the mouse to save the changes, then hit the print button, before turning to face her assistant. She'd prepared a completely revised proposal and, although she still had to trim the budget, it should earn Lawrence's approval before they presented it to Harvey.

"Rumpled clothes, smudged makeup, bloodshot eyes." Neil hummed "Home, home on the range." "I knew you two wouldn't be able to resist each other for long."

"Whoa, whoa." Sonya held up her hand. "It was a rough night, all right. But not in the way you think." Quickly, she filled Neil in on the events of the previous night, except for the part about the kiss. "So, I agreed not to show Rock's face."

"Sweetie, you're completely insane," Neil declared as he sat on a corner of her desk. "Insane, but brilliant."

"Blame the cowboy. He persuaded me to do it."

"Oh?" Neil's eyes gleamed. "And what method of persuasion did he use?"

"His mouth." Sonya ignored the spurt of desire that accompanied her remembrance of Rock's kiss. It'd been too intense, too wild, too…intimate. And primitive compared to the civilized men she'd dated. Rock was just a randy cowboy, out for a good time.

While he might excite her in a purely physical sense, she wasn't here to indulge in personal thrills. No, it'd be best if she kept him at a healthy distance.

"Oooh. Tell all."

She took a long sip of coffee, determined to keep Neil salivating as long as possible. "He talked me into it. So get your mind out of the gutter, Neil."

He pouted. "But life is so much more interesting there."

"We need to focus on the business at hand." She tried to revive her tired eyes by rubbing them. "At least I would, if I were capable of focusing."

Neil tapped his clipboard. "Changing the creative strategy at this point is suicidal."

"I know." Sonya didn't even attempt to stifle the yawn that shuddered through her. She dropped her head into her hands and avoided looking at the papers littering her desk. "I haven't even started on that, yet. I've been adjusting the scheduling as well as the costs of redesigning the whole campaign."

"And?"

"The bad news is we'll probably have to book more studio time than we'd originally planned. That additional cost, plus the extra salaries for the production crew, will put us overbudget. Somehow I have to find a way to shave expenses. The good news is I think we can do it." She straightened up. "It'll mean everyone working their butts off, night and day, for us to have a hope of pulling it off."

Neil nodded. "Done. They might moan and groan a bit, but each one of the crew would walk to hell and back for you." He grinned. "Even if you are insane."

"Thanks. I think."

"That's me, your number one cheerleader. Now, sweetie, what can I do?"

She handed him a pile of paper. "Can you transcribe the notes I made and make sure this gets to the legal department right away?" She stretched. "And schedule a meeting with the creative team for midafternoon. I have a meeting with Lawrence in forty minutes. After that, I'll need you to set up some test shots in the studio. First I'm going to slip back to the hotel for a shower and change of clothes. It shouldn't take me more than half an hour." She checked her watch. "Oh, Neil? Rock will be dropping by shortly for a fitting. Can you look after him for me?"

"I think I'm a big enough boy to look after myself." The now-familiar rasp snagged her frazzled nerves and jump-started her heart. Rock lounged against her door frame. In his simple jade-coloured T-shirt and faded blue jeans he looked damned sexy. And rested.

Neil gave Rock the once-over, then slid her a sidelong glance. "I'm outta here."

"I'll get you for this," she muttered.

Neil smiled and held up her notes. "I have to get working on these." He sidled past Rock, then turned to waggle his fingers at Sonya. "Besides, I think the situation calls for a feminine touch."

The traitor. Sonya forced a tight smile. "Oh, Neil?"

He popped his head back around the door. "Yes, boss lady?"

"You know, I can always make personnel cuts in order to balance the budget."

"Good thing I'm indispensable." He disappeared, whistling the chorus of "Home, home on the Range."

The worst thing was, he was right. Sonya closed her eyes and rubbed her temples.

Rock cleared his throat.

Eyes still closed, she rotated her head, seeking relief for her stiff neck muscles. "You're early." She gasped when two warm hands cradled her neck, then gently kneaded the knots, coaxing them to smooth submissiveness. Those same firm strokes sparked starbursts of sensations that were not appropriate to a business relationship. No matter how good it felt. She reached up and disengaged his hands. "Thank you."

"We've got a problem."

Her eyes snapped open. "I—I agree." She took a deep breath and cranked her head up to look him square in the eyes. "I think it'll help if we refrain from any further physical contact."

A slow smile spread across Rock's face. "That isn't the, uh, problem I was talking about." As he sauntered across to the sitting area of her office, he looked as if he didn't have a care in the world. He sprawled onto her leather sofa, removed his hat and finger-combed his sun-streaked hair, sculpted muscles rippling.

Conscious of her own disheveled appearance and her unwitting admission that his touch affected her, Sonya rose and stalked over to an armchair opposite the sofa. "What then?"

The cowboy quirked an eyebrow in response to the impatience in her voice. "Either you got up on the wrong side of someone's bed—" The dirty look she threw him only deepened the laugh crease that ran down one side of his face. "Nope, I'd say you haven't been to bed at all."

"I had to rework the Rocky Ridge budget." She caught herself trying to smooth out the wrinkles in her dress. Why should she defend her actions and appearance to Rock? She needed to go freshen up and change her clothes, so she could project a professional appearance when she met with Lawrence, and later with Harvey. She'd need all the confidence she could muster to persuade them that the changes to the creative strategy would deliver better-than-promised results for the campaign. She checked her watch. "Can your problem wait until later?"

"No."

"All right, cowboy. You've got five minutes."

"Just now, I had to enter the building through the loading dock." Rock shrugged. "I pretended I was a new addition to the janitorial staff."

As a janitor, he'd have his work cut out for him, all right—mopping up pools of drool from admiring females. "Why on earth would you do that?"

"There's a posse stationed at the front entrance."

"A posse?"

Rock rolled his eyes. "A bunch of reporters."

"Oh." Then the implication of his words sank in. "Good heavens."

"Exactly. You've agreed, in writing, that you'll keep my identity secret. So what are you going to do about it?"

"Nothing."

A puzzled look crossed Rock's face. "If that was meant to reassure me, it didn't work."

Sonya glanced at her watch. "Come with me, and I'll explain it all to you."

"You agreed to what?" Each word, precision cut with Lawrence MacLeod's disdain, punched the funereal silence of the boardroom. The slap of a cigarette case onto the polished surface of the conference table indicated its owner's displeasure.

Clint winced, but, next to him, Sonya didn't flinch. His respect for her grew as he watched her quiet certainty meet the incredulity stamped on the older man's face.

Clint's initial distrust of the too-smooth manner displayed by Sonya's boss escalated to active dislike. He'd seen the same type of personality at work on the skiing circuit, where domineering coaches convinced athletes that they'd never make it on their own. He'd love to shatter MacLeod's condescension with his fist, but was confident Sonya could hold her own in the situation. Besides, he knew if he interfered on behalf of Sonya, his action would instantly destroy her professional credibility. Instead, he'd sit and enjoy watching her handle this egomaniac's thinly masked insults.

"I agreed we'd design the campaign so Rock's face wouldn't be shown."

"Why?" Lawrence flicked his gaze in Clint's direction. "There's nothing wrong with his face."

"The idea is that by not showing his face, we'll develop an extraordinary campaign. By concealing the Rocky Ridge man's identity, we'll create a mystique that will have an incredible impact in the marketplace." Sonya nodded in acknowledgment to Clint. "I want to build on the publicity we've already stimulated with our search for Rock."

"A dangerous tactic."

"A tactic that's demonstrated success, to date."

Lawrence tapped his cigarette case with a manicured finger. "Most likely just a flash in the pan."

"I made a decision that, I believe, is in the best interests of Rocky Ridge blue jeans." Low, but firm, Sonya's voice rang with conviction.

"A disastrous decision." Lawrence's lip curled.

"A decision that's mine to make."

"Unless I decide to relieve you of that responsibility."

Clint noticed Sonya's laced fingers whiten.

"That's certainly your prerogative." Her voice held more than a hint of challenge.

"And I'll exercise it at my discretion."

Lawrence's arrogant sneer and predatory features warned Clint this man liked to wield power solely to his own advantage.

"So, where's the revised contract?"

"Legal will have it ready tomorrow." Sonya flipped open her briefcase. "But I can familiarize you with the changes I've made."

"Good." Lawrence flicked his gaze over Clint. "Maybe it's not too late to impose some level of damage control."

Clint bit back a retort. Sonya didn't need his protection; she didn't need anyone's. Her self-restraint impressed him, as did her problem-solving abilities.

In fact, the lady was fascinating.

She had a natural talent for organizing—demonstrated earlier, when she'd solved the problem of how he could slip into Zenith Communications without the media's knowledge. She'd outlined her idea on the way down the service elevator and through an underground concourse to the hotel complex where she was staying. It was a temporary residence, as different from the permanent home he'd created as night was from day. Obviously, she had no intention of settling down in Calgary.

She'd left him in the lobby while she went to her room to change. It was just as well she hadn't invited him up; the urge to touch her honeyed skin was becoming more difficult to control. When she'd returned in fifteen short minutes, she'd transformed herself from bedroom sexy to boardroom efficient. For some reason, he found that made her even sexier.

Over the past years, his physical needs had been satisfied through an occasional casual relationship. Why should Sonya be any different? There was an attraction between them, no matter how much she might want to deny it. As two consenting adults, they could simply indulge themselves, then go their separate ways. The problem was, Sonya wasn't consenting. Yet. And he couldn't do too much to encourage her. As she'd told him last night, one false move and they were history.

"So, cowboy." Lawrence's pompous tone grated on Clint's nerves. "How do you feel about masquerading as Zenith Communications' new janitor?"

Clint shrugged. "Fine with me. I've rubbed elbows with more than a few laborers, most of which are honest and hardworking. I'd be proud to be considered in their ranks."

Lawrence arched a brow. "The only laborers I know work on my estate. And we don't exactly 'rub elbows.'" With a dismissive gesture, he turned to Sonya. "Let me see the revised schedule and budget."

Sonya passed a file to Lawrence, then met Clint's gaze. Her eyes and facial expression conveyed the apology that Lawrence should have made, but would never recognize as necessary. No wonder the lady had developed such a tough outer shell! She required it to survive the rigors of her daily business life. He could identify with that. He'd had to develop his own skills of survival as a single father and rancher. Thank God his neighbors didn't mind Tia spending so much time with their daughter.

And now he and Sonya, two of the most unlikely allies ever, were dependent upon each other to reach their respective goals. Life was nothing if not ironic.

"You're overbudget." Lawrence sat back with a smirk on his haughty face.

"I know." Sonya worried her lip. "But there're a couple of places where I might come in under projected costs."

"*Might* doesn't cut it. Do it now. I won't let you present this to Harvey unless you achieve a balanced budget."

Sonya's jaw worked as she bent and entered some figures on her calculator. Clint resisted the overwhelming urge to knock her boss onto his pompous ass. She must really love her job to be able to stand working for such a jerk.

"I've already negotiated the best deal for our location shoot at the dude ranch, but if I decrease the number of projected rain dates..." she jotted some figures on the document "...I should be able to bring the expenses down to this."

"Really, Sonya. That's barely a start." Lawrence fit a cigarette into his silver holder. "Since you can't keep this project within budget, I'll have no choice but to find someone who can." With an economy of movement, he lit his cigarette and drew deeply.

Sonya stiffened.

Clint couldn't believe it. Sonya's boss wanted her off this project. The question was why?

"I can rework this budget—I just need a little more time."

She still sounded confident, but, beneath the table, Clint noted a slight tremble in her legs.

MacLeod's moral corruption didn't surprise him. From what Kristin had told him, the industry was rife with it. What bothered him was that Sonya was getting the short end of the stick here.

"As president of the company, it's my responsibility to ensure we protect the investment decision our clients make in hiring our company." Lawrence tapped ashes into a silver ashtray. "I've made no secret of my reservations about how you've handled this account from the beginning."

Stock-still, Sonya stared at her boss.

The bastard was going to pull the plug on her. Anger pounded in Clint's veins. Sonya had said if she succeeded, she'd be vice president of Zenith Communications, one corporate rung below her boss. Then Clint knew. Lawrence wasn't afraid of her failing, he was more afraid of what would happen if Sonya succeeded. Enraged, Clint clenched his jaw. He had to help her.

Sonya locked eyes with her boss. "We have an agreement."

"Oh?" Lawrence blew out a stream of smoke. "Show it to me."

"I—I can't."

Lawrence smirked.

Clint alone held a key that could rescue Sonya, but that very same key had the potential to unlock an even greater disaster for his daughter than losing her home. The choice between sure disaster and potential disaster was an impossible decision, but one he had to make.

"An unsigned piece of paper is useless." Lawrence's smile was thin. "I thought I'd taught you better than that."

The son of a bitch was going to carry out his threat. Sonya blinked, her gaze falling to the papers in front of her. Then, chewing her lip, she glanced at Clint. He'd never seen her look so uncertain.

It was now or never. Clint leaned forward. "I believe I have the solution to your problem."

WITH EACH CLICK of the photographer's camera, Sonya's fury escalated. Under the glare of the studio lights, she noted, the Rocky Ridge blue jeans were molded to Rock's perfect butt. The butt Sonya longed to kick. Instead, she flung imaginary daggers at the rounded target. This whole project was spiraling out of her control, all due to the cowboy.

She hadn't wanted to hire Rock in the first place, but she'd done so. Then she'd been forced into redesigning the whole campaign because she couldn't show his face, and, just a few hours ago, he'd interfered and offered a solution she'd been about to make to her boss. Somehow, she had to retain what little professionalism she had left.

The comfortable chill of Zenith Communications' in-house studio did nothing to cool her fury. Anger throbbed in her chest with each heartbeat. Arms crossed, she watched Neil adjust the flaps on a light.

He turned to her for confirmation. "How's that?"

"Fine," she snapped.

The bustle in the room stilled, as everyone stopped

to look at her. Rock turned, his upper face lost in the shadow of his Stetson.

Neil's eyes widened. "Carry on," he commanded, as he moved to stand beside her.

Cindy, the photographer, hovered around Rock as she continued to measure the light level, laughing and chatting with him. The photographic assistant scurried about, following Cindy's instructions.

Neil leaned closer. "What's wrong?"

Sonya's shoe tapped the cement floor. "Nothing."

"Sweetie, you're like a tiger on the hunt. Who's the lucky victim?"

Rock stepped forward into the golden light. Cindy grasped the waist of his jeans and adjusted the leg seams. Given the wide smile on his face, the cowboy obviously wasn't objecting to the attention.

Sonya couldn't prevent her own face from tightening, her teeth from grinding. The action sent sharp pains shooting through her head.

Neil nodded. "I see."

She pounced on Neil. "Oh? Exactly what do you see?"

"A pair of honey buns that sure fill a pair of jeans." Neil nudged Sonya with his elbow. "Unfortunately, he's not my type."

"I'll tell you what I see," she sputtered in her rage. "An interfering, self-important, rank amateur who—"

"Who just happens to have the best damned buns in western Canada. Right?" Neil put his arm around her shoulders and gave her a quick squeeze. "The buns that can boost your career."

"The buns that saved your butt this afternoon." Rock stood in front of her, hands on his hips.

Her cheeks flooded with heat as she lifted her head to meet his emerald gaze. "The hell you did!"

"Take five, everyone!" Neil scuttled away.

"Then tell me, what the devil happened in that meeting with Lawrence?"

"The usual." Sonya folded her arms across her chest. "Lawrence played the heavy, threatened to remove me from the project. The standard 'can she stand up to the pressure?' routine. He always does that, and he likes it even better when he has a spectator. That's why he invited you to sit in."

"And you put up with that?" Incredulity laced Rock's voice.

She raised her chin, ignoring the intensified pain in her head. "It's good training."

"It sounded pretty real to me."

"I guess it would. He likes to play hardball, to test his executives' negotiating skills." She shrugged. "Actually, this time he did carry it a little further than usual, forcing me to revise the budget on the spot. But before I could give him my solution, you interfered."

He stepped closer. "Really? What were you going to suggest?"

His fresh scent enveloped her. "The same thing you did."

He chucked her chin with one of his lean fingers. "*You* were going to recommend using my ranch for the location shoot?"

Her headache lessened, giving way to a lightheaded sensation. "Well, I had planned on asking you first."

Rock's rich laugh filled the studio. "Damn, you're good!"

The last of her indignation evaporated under the

heat of his admiration. Or was it lust? Her body buzzed from the effects of caffeine, compounded by mental and physical exhaustion. Her knees weakened.

Rock's face moved closer. "It's okay, you know."

Her lips parted. "What is?" she breathed.

"To accept someone else's...help."

If she let him kiss her, in front of half of her production team, she might as well kiss the vice presidency of Zenith Communications goodbye. If she didn't keep herself and this project on track, she wouldn't be worthy of the vice president's position. Sonya collected the last of her reserved strength and stepped back, swaying slightly. She desperately needed an energy boost. As soon as things were under control here, she'd have to slip away and grab a snack. "Let's get back to work, everyone."

"Are you all right?" Rock reached out and grasped her elbow.

"Of course." She shrugged him off and pushed her hair back from her face. "I'm fine. You can take your place."

He frowned, then, without a word, turned and strode back to the set.

Sonya released a sigh of relief. She'd already allowed Rock to have too much influence in her professional life. She'd be damned if she'd permit him the same liberty in her private one. "Neil, what's the next shot?"

"A two-shot of Rock and a female model." Neil smiled as if enjoying a private joke. "We need you to stand in."

Silence roared in her head as Sonya realized that, since the other women had specific jobs to perform, she was the only available female in the room. She'd lose more than she'd gain if she insisted a secretary be brought in—even though that's what her instinct for self-preservation prodded her to do. And she couldn't plead she was too fatigued; she'd just told Rock she was fine—even though her head felt stuffed with sodden cotton wool. "Sure. I'm game."

"Great." Cindy consulted her clipboard. "This is the shot where Rock and the model embrace."

"Just my luck," Sonya muttered under her breath. The memory of last night's intoxicating kiss assaulted her. As she relived the devastating sensations that had been unleashed by Rock's lips, heat prickled her skin. His presumptuous behavior had been bad enough, but what had been even more unacceptable was her own reckless response. One violation of business protocol was one too many. She couldn't allow things to get out of hand again.

"Rock, take your mark." Cindy gestured to the tape on the floor. He stepped into place. "Sonya, please stand in front of him."

As she moved from the obscurity of the shadows onto the edge of the set, the dizzying glare of the lights renewed her throbbing headache. Sonya stopped and shut her eyes.

"Want to borrow my hat?" Rock teased.

"No, thanks." Shading her eyes with one hand, Sonya tried to ignore the glimmer of amusement in the cowboy's gaze. But she couldn't ignore the surge in her pulse as she closed the distance between them.

"Step right into him," Cindy urged.

Rock's laugh crease deepened as he opened his arms in invitation. "I won't bite." As Sonya stopped, her body mere inches from his, he lowered his arms, tucked his thumbs in his belt loops and added in a rough whisper, "Unless you want me to."

A humming awareness enclosed them in its invisible cocoon.

Struggling to maintain her equilibrium, Sonya attempted a cool smile. "All I want is to get this over with."

The cowboy simply grinned.

"Sonya, can you put your arm, the one farthest from the camera, around Rock's neck?"

Lifting her leaden limb, Sonya braced her forearm on Rock's strong shoulder, careful to keep as much space as possible between her breast and his chest. The less contact, the better. Averting her face from him, she fixed her eyes on Cindy.

"Rock, put your far arm around Sonya's upper back and the other one around her waist," Cindy directed.

As Rock's firm arms closed around her, Sonya flinched from the shivers of awareness that radiated from his touch. In defense, she locked her spine into a perfectly vertical position.

"Comfy?"

"Perfectly," she hissed.

"Liar."

She'd die before admitting to him just how uncomfortable she was. The intense heat of the lights thickened the air and threatened to rob her lungs of oxygen. Drawing a deep breath, she inhaled a potent dose of Rock's male scent. Her nerve endings sprang to an instant alert.

"Great," Cindy enthused. She peered into the camera. "Okay, Sonya, put your other hand on Rock's derriere."

Sonya stared at Cindy and tried to summon a good reason to refuse the instruction. But reason had deserted her.

"Not up to the challenge?" Rock purred.

She couldn't back down now. "This isn't a challenge." Leaning forward, she clapped her hand against the curve of his derriere. "This is business."

"Business before pleasure?"

"Just business."

Rock adjusted his stance and, beneath her splayed fingers, a muscle in his backside quivered. The small intimacy released a major surge of desire. Only denim separated her palm from his bare flesh. Her hand grew moist.

"Perfect. Now move closer together." Cindy pushed them into a clutch position.

The move aligned Sonya's hips flush with Rock's groin. In moments his heat permeated the silk of her dress, gluing it to her damp skin. Their sensual pose evoked a feminine response so strong it sucked her breath away. She longed to surrender, to let go and allow him to support her sluggish body. But she couldn't give in to the temptation. In an effort to minimize contact, she held herself rigid, gritting her teeth against the strain.

"It'll be a whole lot easier if you don't fight this," he murmured into her ear. "Just relax against me."

His warm breath feathered caresses down her neck, sending shivers down her braced spine. "In your dreams, cowboy."

His chest rumbled. "Been there, done that."

"Okay, hold it."

With excruciating slowness, Cindy returned to her camera and relayed instructions to the lighting technicians. Sonya defied the spasms of her protesting muscles.

"Okay, guys, can you look at each other?"

Turning her head, Sonya found herself nose-to-nose with Rock. Lust smoldered in the jade depths of his eyes, while evidence of his arousal bulged against her abdomen. She fought a smothering sensation of desire.

"Give him a seductive smile, Sonya."

Rock's mouth hovered close. Too close. There was no air. Just intense heat. And Rock.

"Fantastic. Just tilt your head back a little."

Immediately, a wave of dizziness engulfed her.

"Sonya? Are you okay?"

Rock's face wavered above hers. Without warning, her muscles melted and thought slipped away as she surrendered to inky darkness.

7

A WARM HAND STROKED Sonya's cheek, brushing her hair back from her face. Only her grandmother had ever touched her with such tenderness. Drowsy, she cuddled into the warmth, comforted by the steady heartbeat beneath her ear. It took a couple of moments for instinct to nudge her. The arms cradling her were iron-hard, not frail, and the chest—which was hard, not soft—smelled of spice, not lavender. And her grandmother was buried in Heavenly Acres Cemetery.

Suspicion grew into fact when Sonya opened her eyes to a wall of green T-shirt. Blinking, she looked up to find a gentle smile on Rock's face. Her headache had diminished to a dull ache.

"So, that's what they mean by an executive power nap."

Heat flushed her face. "Tell me I didn't pass out in front of my staff. Please tell me it didn't happen."

"Okay." His thumb rubbed the ridge of her cheekbone. "It didn't happen."

"Liar," she whispered.

Rock laid a finger on her lips. "Shh."

He was sitting on her office sofa with one hand tangled in her hair, and she was curled onto his lap like a fawning cat. His other muscular arm was wrapped around her back, his hand on the swell of her hip.

Insanity.

She had to be insane. It was the only possible reason why, in the middle of the day, she was lounging in a man's lap. And not just any man's—Rock's. And what was really insane was that she was turned on. Incredibly turned on. Just as she had been in the studio, just as she had been last night, just as she had been since she'd first seen him. She was becoming a lust slave. To a cowboy.

She'd have to worry about the repercussions of that later. Right now, she had a job to do. Stifling a groan, she tried to sit up. Her head vibrated with a burst of dizziness.

"Whoa, there. You're as pale as a ghost." His strong arms held her in place. "You're staying right here."

"I can't. We need to finish the test shots, then I have a meeting—"

"Let Neil take care of the shoot. The meeting can wait." Rock cupped her chin, his green eyes serious. "You need to rest for a while, or you'll take another nosedive. Then people might think you're really falling for me."

His thumb traced her lips, its intimate promise nourishing the need he'd aroused. Desire, thick and molten, stirred her very core. She nipped his thumb with her teeth. "Hardly."

"Liar." His eyes darkened as he lowered his face to hers, cupping her face with his hands.

He caressed her lips with a whisper-soft kiss, then withdrew. A heartbeat later, he brushed them again. And again. With each touch, her greed for more grew. Her lips parted in invitation; her hand stole to the nape of Rock's neck and tangled in his hair, melding their lips together. She tasted his ripe passion and fed it with her own.

She thrilled to the evidence of his urgent arousal, her blood heating in response. His hand stroked her hip, her thigh. She undid a button on his shirt, her hand slipping inside to graze the hard muscles of his chest. So firm, so...male.

His own hand explored the curve of her waist, the dips in her rib cage, the swell of her breast. Wild sensations erupted as his thumb skimmed her nipple, plump with desire. She whimpered with pleasure.

Growling in response, Rock shifted her onto the sofa, holding his body over hers. His lips nuzzled her neck, pausing to kiss the skin above her hammering pulse. Her body craved fulfillment. A recklessness she'd never experienced seized her, urging her to succumb. The very idea was titillating. Though control was central to her survival, the temptation to surrender completely to the seduction of pure passion was...potent.

He reclaimed her lips, slowly lowering his body onto hers, and she arched to meet him. Something sharp dug into her abdomen—his belt buckle. She smiled. Well, that was easily taken care of. Her seeking hand closed around the object, a large disk of braided metal. Her mother had worn an identical disk on a chain around her neck.

A rodeo buckle.

Insanity.

Sonya's desire evaporated.

"Stop." She whispered. "Please."

At first, when her body slackened, Clint thought she'd fainted again. When he opened his eyes and saw her tormented expression, he almost wished she had. He cupped her face in his hands. "Sonya, what's wrong?"

"You. Me." Her voice became choked. "This."

Taking a deep breath, he inched back from the sharp edge of desire. She'd wanted him. He'd seen it in her eyes, felt it in her body. God knew he craved her. Clint could have taken her, right there on her office sofa, and would have if she hadn't stopped him.

Her vulnerability staggered him. Vulnerability signaled danger, intense emotional involvement. He'd seen, firsthand, the evidence of its destructive power. In Kristin.

Lust he could handle. Anything else was unacceptable, idiotic.

He and Sonya had wanted each other; that was an undeniable fact. But something had made her change her mind. *Fool.* He was the reason. She'd fainted, and when she came to, he'd rushed her in a haze of hormones.

They would indulge their craving later, when they were both ready for it. Then, when their time was up, they'd part as two adults who'd satisfied their mutual needs. No more, no less. No involvement, no regrets. On either side.

He sat at the opposite end of the sofa, unsure of what to say. "Can I get you something?"

"No. Thanks." She started to sit up, but fell back, bracing her head in her hands.

"What's wrong?"

She kept her eyes closed. "I'm a little dizzy, that's all."

"When did you last eat?"

"I—I'm not sure." She frowned. "There've been so many details to take care of the past few days." She rubbed her forehead with her fingers. "I had an oatmeal muffin yesterday morning. Since then, I guess I've been feeding off adrenaline."

"Good God, woman." He raked a hand through his hair. "You had no sleep last night and nothing to eat for a day and a half? You need to start looking after yourself."

She tilted her chin. "I've been doing that since I was seventeen."

He frowned his concern. "What about your family?"

She shrugged. "My mother died when I was eleven." Her voice softened as she added, "Then I lived with my grandmother for six years, until she passed away. After that, I was on my own."

No wonder she found it so hard to relinquish her self-sufficiency. She'd had no other choice. "What about your father?"

Her eyes avoided his. "I have no father." As if aware of the sharpness of her voice, she forced a smile. "What is this, an inquisition?"

Before Clint could probe further, a soft knock sounded. Neil stuck his head around the edge of the door, his face wrinkled with anxiety. "How is she?"

"I'm fine," she insisted.

"No, she isn't." Sonya tried to sit up again, but Clint restrained her. "She needs something to eat." He waved Neil over. "You stay right here with her."

Neil nodded, picked up one of Sonya's hands and began massaging it. "Poor baby."

She pulled her hand away. "Really, Neil, I'm all right."

Clint scanned her pale face, noting the shadows of exhaustion under her eyes. "Give Neil instructions for the shoot. I'm going to get you some half-decent food."

"But I—"

He pointed a finger at her. "If you so much as move a muscle, I swear I'll hog-tie you."

"You wouldn't dare."

"Don't tempt me."

Neil snickered.

Clint sent him a warning glance. "If she moves, you'll answer to me."

"Hey, big guy." Neil raised his hands in mock surrender. "No need to be hostile—I'm on your side." He plucked a tissue from the nearby table. "Here, you might need this."

Clint frowned in silent question.

"Lipstick smudges."

"Thanks." Clint wiped his mouth. Satisfied, he nodded and shifted his gaze to Sonya. "Behave."

She glared in defiance. "Brute."

Her voice was too weak to carry much sting, but the lady was one headstrong filly. Luckily, one of the first things he'd learned as a rancher, then later as a father, was the trick of managing a wilful nature without sacrificing the beauty of its spirit. He smiled. "Honey, you ain't seen nothin' yet."

Neil waited until the door closed behind Rock. "Oooh. How deliciously Neanderthal. Tell me everything. Don't leave out a single detail."

In the absence of Rock's body heat, the coolness of the leather sofa seeped through Sonya's silk dress. She shivered. "Neil, if you have a shred of decency, you'll hand me the jacket hanging on the back of my chair and get me some headache tablets from the top right-hand drawer of my desk."

"Of course, sweetie." He patted her hand. "But since my shred of decency is pretty flimsy, I'll only do it if you promise to fill me in on what's happening with you and Rock."

What's happening with you and Rock. Put that way, it sounded so sordid, so…unprofessional. How had she let the whole situation slip out of her control? She shook her head. "There's nothing to tell."

"Come on. I was in the studio. The two of you were ready to combust." He handed her the jacket. "And when I came in here, there was guilt written all over your faces. And lipstick."

She shrugged her jacket on and pulled it tight around her.

"You two made out, didn't you?" Neil clapped his hands. "I knew it."

"We did not!"

"So you kissed a little."

Shame curled Sonya's shoulders. "Despite the fact I don't even know if he's married or not, it was inappropriate. I'm an employee of Zenith Communications, and I'm contracting him to do work with us. That makes us business associates. A relationship with him could be corporate suicide."

"Sweetie. I think you're being a little hard on yourself. This isn't the Middle Ages."

"Come on, Neil. I'm not a prude, but there's a double standard out there. If I were a man having an affair with a female model, the other guys would slap me on the back and call me lucky. But since I'm a woman, you can bet they'd whisper behind my back and call me a tramp."

Neil's face sobered. "You can't live your life by other people's standards."

"You do if you want to be vice president of Zenith Communications. Can you imagine what Lawrence's reaction would have been if he'd walked in?"

"Mmm. He'd have gotten an education, all right. Lust is in the air every time you and Rock get within sight of each other. But you're right, next time I'd choose another location."

Her body still tingled from the sensations Rock had evoked; the rich anticipation of fulfillment hadn't fully faded. "There's not going to be a next time."

"You're making a big mistake, sweetie." Neil released a gusty sigh. "For what it's worth, here's my advice. Let Lawrence dictate the rules in the boardroom, but not in your bedroom." He leaned forward. "Personally, I think you give too much of yourself to the job."

"It's all I have."

"What happens if it disappears?" He touched her cheek. "You've got to learn to live a little, Sonya."

Gritty memories of her childhood assaulted her. Nights punctuated with loud country music and raucous laughter; drunken cowboys lurching out of the apartment in the early morning.... She shuddered. "I'm living the life I want."

"You're not your mother."

With the wanton way she'd responded to the cowboy, Sonya wasn't so sure. Fear licked, deep and hot. "No. I won't allow myself to be."

THE NEXT AFTERNOON, Sonya sat at her desk, reviewing her copy of the final draft of Rock's contract. After a good night's sleep, she'd awakened refreshed, yesterday's nightmare events a distant memory. She'd certainly learned her lesson. Since she didn't want to end up like her mother, from now on she'd make sure to eat properly and get her rest.

After Rock had ordered a three-course meal for her from room service, he and Neil had left to finish the test shots. She'd devoured every morsel, then met briefly with her creative team. Satisfied they were on schedule, she'd taken her laptop back to her room and completed the revisions on the budget and creative strategy for the Rocky Ridge advertising campaign. Only then had she allowed herself the luxury of a twelve-hour sleep.

Today Sonya Duncan, senior account executive, was back on track. One thing she knew was that when Rock came in to sign the contract, she'd have to thank him for all he'd done. Despite his heavy-handed manner, he'd been very sweet. Gentle, even. Unexpectedly so, for a cowboy. Still, she'd have to make sure he understood that her behaviour yesterday had been quite irrational, quite out of character.

He'd made her body come alive in ways no one else ever had. But he was still a virtual stranger. For all she knew, he was a two-timing married rogue. Other women might fall for his rugged charm, but the few lovers she'd accepted into her bed had been carefully selected. She had no time, or inclination, to get involved with anyone. Her work was her passion.

He'd better not be under the impression that he could snap his fingers and she'd melt at his feet. *If* she decided to indulge her insanity and sleep with the cowboy—as unlikely as that was—it'd be on *her* terms. No one else's.

The problem was she hadn't discouraged his advances yesterday; in fact, she'd encouraged him. Something within her had responded to his tenderness. It was a powerful elixir that might lead to incurable addiction. And it scared her to death. She needed time to think things through.

The best strategy would be to reestablish a proper business relationship—cool and distant. She snapped the contract back into its file folder.

"Hi."

The simple syllable vibrated with hidden meaning, serving both as a salutation and an invitation.

With a sedate smile, she ignored the invitation. "Hi, there." She tapped her watch. "You're early. Again."

"One of my better bad habits."

"I shudder to know the worst."

Rock checked over his shoulder, tiptoed forward, then whispered loudly, "I've been known to squeeze the toothpaste from the middle of the tube."

The intimate thought of him in his bathrobe, his hair tousled from sleep, stole into her mind. Was there a woman who shared the bathroom...and his bed? Sonya lifted a nonchalant brow. "That must drive your wife crazy."

The humor fled from his face, leaving it hard, closed. "I don't have a wife."

Sonya retreated from the discomfort she'd uncovered in him and in herself. "Not that it's any of my business." At least she hadn't almost given herself to a married man. Then who was the mystery woman he was protecting? A girlfriend? A lover? To break the ensuing silence, she shuffled some papers.

"Sonya."

He leaned over the front of her desk, golden hair glinting on his strong, tanned forearms. His long, brown fingers rested against white papers, the same fingers that had held her yesterday, that had caressed her with such passion. Her heart kicked into hyperdrive. Reluctantly, she raised her head. The intensity in his eyes fed her involuntary response, heightening her awareness of his potent masculinity.

"I want to see you tonight."

Alarm bells pealed in her head. Not a good idea. She looked up to find his lips inches from hers. He smelled of sunlight, warm male musk and coffee. Desire rolled in thick, honeyed waves. She pressed back in her chair and licked her dry lips. "I can't. I have work to catch up on."

"We need to talk about what happened yesterday."

"There's nothing to say. It was a mistake and it won't happen again."

The heat in his gaze flickered.

"Sorry to make this duo a trio." Neil breezed in. "The big brass are in the boardroom, waiting to sign the contract." He dropped a packet on her desk. "Here are the proofs from the test shots."

Sonya scooped up some files and handed them to her assistant. "Can you escort Rock to the boardroom? I'll be right there. I just need a moment to freshen up."

"I know where it is." Rock swiveled and strode out of the office, with Neil trailing behind.

Relief rocketed through her. That had been close. Too close. Neil had been right about one thing—there was an incredible sexual energy between her and the cowboy. Right now, distance was the only cure.

A couple of minutes in the washroom with her comb and lipstick gave her a much-needed respite. When she entered the boardroom, Sonya felt Rock's penetrating stare. She took a seat to the right of

Lawrence, almost directly across the table from the cowboy. Following greetings, Lawrence gave a little speech and directed the signing procedure with all the aplomb of a victorious general.

After congratulatory handshakes all around, Lawrence popped the cork on a bottle of chilled champagne and handed a champagne flute to each of them. "We have a double celebration today: the opening of Zenith Communications' Calgary office and the signing of the Rocky Ridge man." He raised his flute. "To Sonya and Rock."

They all clinked glasses and drank.

"I also want to take the opportunity to make a special toast to Sonya. She's designed a daring advertising campaign and insisted I give her independent status on the entire Rocky Ridge project. I salute her initiative and trust she'll make us all proud." He touched his glass to hers, gave a slight bow and raised the pale gold liquid to his lips. Above the rim, his blue eyes were cool, watchful.

Survival of the smartest. Sonya should have anticipated this move. Lawrence had just upped the ante by publicly placing the sole responsibility for the Rocky Ridge project on her shoulders. In doing so, he'd positioned himself to receive some credit for success and deny any culpability for failure. She squared her shoulders. She wouldn't fail. Whatever it took to prove him wrong, she'd do it. She'd work night and day, if necessary, to mold the cowboy. She'd prove to one and all she was worthy of the vice presidency.

Harvey came over and flung a beefy arm around her. "I know you won't let me down, little lady."

Lawrence plucked the champagne from its silver bucket and replenished his glass. "Normally, I'd take everyone out to dinner, but Harv and I are off to Vegas for a couple of days. Sonya, you'll take Rock to dinner on our behalf, won't you?"

Regardless of her personal apprehension about being in an intimate situation with Rock, professional courtesy demanded an instant, and positive, reply. She'd ensure their conversation centered on business and she'd take the opportunity to begin tutoring him in the finer skills of media presentation. She pasted the requisite smile on her face. "Of course. It would be my pleasure."

"Thank you for the offer." Rock set his champagne flute down on the table. "But I'll have to pass on it."

His answer stunned Sonya. Only a short while ago, he'd asked to get together with her. Since his invitation had been a personal request, she'd been compelled to turn it down, but this was different. This was business. Was it his intent to embarrass her by refusing Lawrence's directive? "Why?"

Rock raised his eyebrows. "I'm sure you agree it wouldn't be wise for us to be seen in public together." He held up his copy of the contract. "Otherwise, it could ruin our plan to keep the identity of the Rocky Ridge man a secret."

His cool reminder was like a slap in the face. She'd been so careful up until now, even going so far as to require anyone involved in the campaign to sign a confidentiality agreement. She'd allowed her emotions to distract her from her responsibilities. "Of course."

"That's easily solved." Lawrence waved a dismissive hand. "Sonya can entertain you in her suite. It'll give you an opportunity to discuss the details for the location shoot."

"Excellent idea," Harvey exclaimed. "You can mix business with pleasure."

There would be no pleasure on tonight's menu, Sonya vowed. Only business.

WHAT THE HELL was he doing? As the mahogany and brass elevator whisked him up to the twenty-third floor of the hotel complex, Clint debated the wisdom of keeping this imposed dinner date.

Yesterday, he'd almost taken advantage of Sonya's vulnerability. It wasn't an action he was proud of. His unfettered desire had caused him to lose sight of the fact that his first priority should be the Rocky Ridge advertising campaign, not his libido.

Last night, he'd decided his only option would be to apologize and to suggest they restrict themselves to a business-only relationship.

That's why he'd originally asked to see her tonight. In her office this afternoon, Sonya had also made it quite clear that a physical relationship between them was out of the question.

They both had too much to lose. The money he'd received for signing the contract had made only a slight dent in what he owed the bank. Plus Sonya had enough to worry about with that idiot MacLeod breathing down her neck. She didn't need Clint doing the same. No matter how much her delectable neck tempted him.

It was past time for him to practice some self-control. Raising his hand, he knocked on the door to her suite.

When the door opened, a fantasy of pure sensual elegance greeted his eyes. The neckline of Sonya's curve-hugging bronze dress exposed an expanse of creamy skin that begged to be caressed. His testosterone level soaring, he clung to the edge of self-control. There were limits to the sensual torture even he could endure.

"Hi." Her smile was cool, her manner reserved.

Given the circumstances, the evening would be awkward, a strained exercise in social niceties. He'd be better off going home, relieving the baby-sitter and relaxing with his daughter. He gave Sonya the large gift box he carried, careful not to touch her. "Look, I don't think dinner is such a good idea, after all. Why don't we leave it until another time?"

She looked at the parcel, then gave him a wary look. "What's this?"

She had every right to be suspicious of his motives. "A thank-you present."

Confusion clouded her amber eyes. "A thank-you present for what?"

"For having faith in my potential, and respect for my privacy, despite your misgivings about both."

She stared, her surprise evident.

That irked him even more than her wariness. Not that he could blame her. To date, he hadn't given her much evidence of his self-restraint. Palming the crown of his Stetson, he settled it on his head. He pulled a map from his back pocket and passed it to her. "Let me know when you want to tour the ranch."

"You're leaving?"

"Look, you've been obliged to play hostess tonight." He shrugged. "I have no desire to force myself on you."

"Wait." Her eyes searched his, then she stepped

back and opened the door wider. "Come in, Rock. Please. We've got a lot of work to do. I'd like to start by reviewing the proofs of yesterday's test shots with you."

8

SONYA SET THE GIFT BOX and map on a side table. "Would you like a drink of vermouth?"

The perfect muscle relaxant. Clint removed his Stetson and set it beside the box. "Please. I'm surprised you remembered." The thought warmed him inside. Since they couldn't be lovers, perhaps they could be friends. Not only was it safer, but after MacLeod's declaration this afternoon, it looked like the lady could use all the allies she could get.

"It's a rather unusual drink."

He worded his reply so as not to reveal too much information about his past. "I, uh, traveled a lot in my impressionable youth. A buddy of mine in France introduced me to that particular poison."

"I'd love to see France some day, especially Paris." She handed him a tumbler, careful to hold it so their hands didn't touch. "I travel, but not for pleasure."

"You have to be careful not to let your work consume you." Like Kristin had. "Take time to enjoy some of the finer things in life." He saluted her with his glass, then sipped the clear liquid. The dual tasks of controlling his physical response and monitoring how much information he revealed increased the awkward undercurrents between them.

Her back turned to him, she poured a glass of white

wine. "So I've been told. Do you travel much these days?"

"No. The ranch keeps me pretty busy." Eager to steer the attention away from himself, he took quick stock of her suite. "Nice place you have here."

The muted decor reflected the image its occupant liked to project—beautiful, but cool. In the dining area, a table had been set for two. Snowy linen was accented by a dusky rose cloth, while crystal stemware and silver flatware gleamed. There were no personal knickknacks, no photos, nothing out of place.

She shrugged. "It suits my needs. It's close to work and, if all goes as planned, I'll be back in the Toronto head office in a few months."

For some reason, the thought unsettled him. He strolled through a pair of sliding doors, onto a balcony that overlooked the Bow River. A slight breeze stirred the warm, dense air, while bearded thunderheads advanced like an army of hunchbacked soldiers. There'd be a thunderstorm before the night was through. He'd promised Tia he'd be home in time, so they could watch nature's spectacle. It was a tradition they'd started when she was little and climbed into his lap to hide from the storm. Now they both looked forward to sitting side by side on the veranda, as thunder boomed overhead and lightning streaked across the face of the mountains. God, he loved this country.

Catching a whiff of Sonya's subtle perfume as she moved to stand beside him, he stifled the urge to gather her into his arms. This could prove to be a taxing friendship. He'd never lusted after any other friend this way.

"Where is your ranch?"

He pointed out the direction. "About fifty kilometers that way. I've got a few hundred hectares nestled against the foothills. Good cattle country."

She squinted toward the distant mountains. "Will you be able to save it?"

"As long as I get the balance of my fee."

"You'll get it right after we finish the final shooting." She held up her glass. "Here's to a successful completion of the campaign."

"I'll second that." He touched the rim of his glass to hers. "When would you like to take the grand tour of the ranch?"

"How about the day after tomorrow?"

"Sure. I'll pick you up at nine."

"Great." She took a sip of her wine. "I've never been on a ranch before."

"Where'd you grow up?"

She hesitated for a moment, then gestured to the city. "I was born here in Calgary, but we moved a lot throughout western Canada, from city to city, town to town."

"You and your mother?"

"Mmm."

"Why did you move so much?"

Her chin jutted. "My mother served tables in country-and-western bars. She'd once been a singer, but..." Sonya pivoted toward the open French doors. "Why don't we take a look at those test photos? Later, we can order dinner."

Clint followed her inside, disappointed by her reluctance to share the sadness and grief that he'd detected there. She fascinated him, this quick-minded woman who commanded respect in business, yet who was so tight-lipped about her personal life. He admired her incredible personal strength, her resilience. Taken in context, the vulnerability she'd displayed yesterday had been an aberration, not a character flaw. The urge to comfort her remained. He sighed. If only things were simpler between them. If they'd met under different circumstances, they'd have been lovers by now. There was no doubt in his mind.

As Sonya led Rock to the entertainment area of the suite, she wondered why she'd been so tempted to open up to him about her past. In some ways, it would be so easy to let him into her life. Her resolve had begun to weaken when she'd opened her door and had seen him standing there. In his black denim jeans and black western shirt, he'd reminded her of a magnificent stallion, all sinuous muscle and restrained power. It was more than his breathtaking physique, more than his rugged charm, more than his unexpected tenderness and compassion. It was all those, plus his sincerity, his integrity.

She'd seen the desire in Rock's eyes, yet he'd been willing to walk away. Perhaps she should have let him.

His declaration that he wasn't there to force himself on her had relieved her. So why had it also disappointed her? Surely it would be best to keep their relationship platonic; that way they could work more comfortably together, without distraction. Except it would be difficult to put the idea into practice. Her whole body went on awareness alert whenever the cowboy was near.

Rock picked up the gift box from the side table and gave it to her. "You forgot to open your present."

Cautious of surprises, Sonya gingerly removed the

gold-edged bow and beautiful wrapping paper. Lifting the lid of the box, she discovered a snowy-white Stetson. The cowboy hat jerked her back to her childhood, back to the days when she'd snuggled on her mother's lap and listened to the glorious stories of her cowboy father. She'd coveted a Stetson, somehow believing it would bring her unknown father closer. Later, when she'd grown old enough to understand the coarse nature of the endless string of cowboys her mother brought home, she'd grown to hate the symbol of the West.

Today, she wasn't sure of her feelings. "Thank you." Her hand trembled as she stroked the firm crown. "It's lovely."

She placed it on an end table next to the sofa, determined to get down to business. A large magnifying glass and several contact sheets were spread out on the coffee table. Kicking off her shoes, she knelt on the floor and gestured to Rock. "We got some really good shots. Do you want to take a look?"

She held the magnifying glass over one of the tiny photos, determined not to allow her hand to tremble. Kneeling down beside her, he leaned forward, his shoulder brushing hers. The resulting impact slammed her senses, and an echoing tremor caused the photo to wobble. His hand closed over hers, steadying the magnifying glass, but the action only increased the severity of the rippling shock waves that eroded her willpower. Her breathing became constricted.

"What is it you look for?"

His lips were only inches from hers. She moistened her own and strove for a businesslike tone. "Body language, a certain attitude." She pointed to the photo in question. "See the perpendicular lines created by your shoulders and chest? That conveys conviction, your wide-legged stance indicates strength, your hands on your hips shout a challenge."

Conscious of the heat building between their bodies, she repositioned the magnifying glass. "See the difference here? The sloping shoulder, the thumb tucked into the belt loop project a totally different mood, of nonchalance. A forward lean could indicate friendliness, a certain tilt of the head an invitation. The trick is to visually convey an emotion through your body language, and to dramatize the effect with the use of shadow."

He moved the magnifying glass to another photo. "What is the purpose of this one?"

It was the photo taken just prior to her collapse. She swallowed. "The intent is to project the emotion the female model feels when she touches the...perfect Rocky Ridge derriere."

Rock turned his head to hers, his eyes a deep jade green, his lips a heartbeat away. "What emotion is that?"

"Lust," she breathed. His potent male scent seduced her senses, evoking a pure feminine response she was incapable of resisting. Caught in the invisible web of their mutual desire, she trembled as his head lowered to hers.

His mouth closed on hers, his magic enfolding her.

Clint kissed her with a hunger born of denial, a passion spurred by need. Cupping her head, his greedy lips devoured hers, discovering every lush nuance. He wanted to lose himself in Sonya, to forget all about mortgages, responsibilities and media people. He wanted to indulge in simple physical satisfaction.

When Sonya wrapped her arms around his neck, leaned into him and invited him to deepen the kiss, his blood roared. He drank her honeyed sweetness, more intoxicating than any liquor, more exhilarating than the pure air and sunshine at the top of a mountain peak on a brilliant winter's day. His fingertips skimmed the slant of her back and she arched into him, her breasts crushed against his rib cage, her abdomen pressed against his robust arousal.

Desire thundered in Clint's veins, summoning him to the precipice of a seductive slope, full of dangerous promise. He craved to plunge headlong, to taste all of Sonya's textures, caress her hidden curves and experience her expanse of creamy skin.

However, he'd learned the hard way the value of slow exploration, the necessity to first meander down the mountain, to judge its attitude. For the unsuspecting, the simple thrill of speed could lead to deadly results. The expert learned to respect, not to conquer; to balance safety with risk.

The challenge would be to survive, emotionally intact. But Sonya affected him like no woman ever had. Already it might be too late.

Before reason completely deserted him, he dragged his mouth from hers. Her amber eyes opened, fire smoldering in their depths. "Sonya." He cupped her oval face in his hands. "If you don't want this, tell me now."

"I want you, cowboy." Her murmur throaty with desire, she drew his lips back to hers. He needed no further urging.

Sonya exulted in the marvelous freedom of spontaneity. Why hadn't she heeded Neil's advice to seize the moment sooner? Because she'd never met anyone like Rock before.

Regardless of how little she knew about him, instinct told her she could trust him. He wasn't tainted with the same character as the coarse cowboys who'd taken advantage of her mother. Rock wouldn't use her, then drop her like a used rag. They'd reach mutual consensus when their time was up. Although her previous lovers had been carefully selected, the liaisons had been short-term. Any hint of emotional involvement and she'd terminated them. Despite that, she'd never permitted the impulse of a one-night stand.

Besides, her circumstances were entirely different from her mother's. Sonya had control of her life, a successful career, independence—all of the things that, in her emotional weakness, her mother had lost. Instead, Sonya was walking into this affair with her eyes open. It promised exactly what she wanted: great sex, with no emotional residue.

Her senses swam with the sumptuous craving aroused by the cowboy's rock-hard body. He tasted earthy and wild, yet his lips promised heavenly pleasures. Her fingers roamed his back, marveling at the sculpted planes, the corded muscles. Rock was solid, steadfast—not the type to take his satisfaction, then stumble out in the middle of the night, but someone who'd be there in the morning.

She hoped.

Sensations erupted as his hands skimmed her back from her neck to her hips. Then his head was bending, raining warm kisses down her neck, pausing to nuzzle the sensitive point above her collarbone where her pulse pounded in anticipation. While his mouth traced the plunging vee of her dress, his hands skimmed up her waist to her rib cage and feathered across her straining breasts. She moaned as a tide of elemental lust ripped through her entire body.

She reveled in sensation as her dress fluttered to the floor. His shirt and jeans joined her clothing in glorious abandonment.

His intimate gaze worshiped her as she stood, clad only in scraps of flesh-colored silk. From deep inside, an unfamiliar eroticism pounded in a primitive pulse. A bold, reckless desire engulfed her. She pressed against his bronzed body, so hard and lean, divested him of his briefs and, stroking his engorged shaft, guided him onto the sofa.

"Wait." He opened his hand and revealed a packaged condom.

She raised an eyebrow.

"Always be prepared."

She took the silver packet. "Allow me."

Straddling Rock, she sheathed him, then sampled the dark wonder of his mouth, tasted the sheen of salt on his sculpted chest and feathered kisses on the gnarled flesh beneath his rib cage. His shudders and groans fed her impetuous power. She rubbed his heat against the silken barrier that concealed her core, gasping when his hot mouth closed over her silk-clad nipple, his tongue flicking its sensitive peak.

She arched her back and rocked against him as sheer wantonness drove her higher, higher, the spirals of desire tightening, intensifying. She strained at the pinnacle, then soared heavenward on pulsating waves of midnight velvet.

Satisfaction and desire surged through Clint as he witnessed her orgasm. He tugged the silk aside and penetrated her slick heat, driving into her spasms. She moaned, tightening around him, her fingers raking his hair, her mouth fastening on his, stoking his desire, as their bodies lurched together in a primal rhythm.

His hands caressed her satiny flesh, his need fueled by her abandon, the intense pressure building, escalating until she convulsed around him. Her contractions shattered his control, wringing his own shuddering release. Forehead to forehead, they collapsed into each other. Between gasps of air, they plucked kisses from one another's lips as their racing heartbeats diminished.

Clint cupped her face as an enigmatic emotion gripped his heart. "Lady, you sure know how to entertain."

A cat-got-the-cream smile lit up her face. She tilted her head and trailed a finger down his cheek, skimming his laugh crease. "And you're quite the guest, cowboy."

They shared languid kisses until he pulled her head onto his chest. Clint palmed a bare and perfect shoulder. "Was this part of the business you'd planned for tonight?"

She smiled up at him. "No, it was an on-the-spot executive decision."

"Boy, I'm sure glad I was on the spot...with the right executive."

With an exquisite gentleness, one of Sonya's fingertips explored the mangled tissue of his scar. "What happened?"

He debated giving her an evasive answer, but instead met her somber gaze and told the truth. "I had a serious skirmish with a ski pole a few years ago."

She shimmied down and dusted the deformity with satiny kisses. "I wish I'd been there to nurse your injury."

So did he. Kristin had made no secret of her revulsion of the wound and had taken great pains never to touch it. The accident that ended his competitive skiing career had also signaled the decline of their intimacy, the decay of their marriage. In the end, Tia had been the only bond that kept them together.

Touched by Sonya's compassion, Clint drew her up and embraced her. "There's another casualty of battle that could use some tender loving care," he teased.

With soft, sultry strokes, Sonya caressed his swelling need. "I'd say it's recovering quite rapidly." Her teeth nipped at his earlobe.

"Now that you mention it…" He nibbled at her lower lip while unfastening and removing her bra. When he trailed the tip of his tongue down to her pebbled nipple, she twisted her fingers in his hair and whimpered with desire.

Limbs tangling, mouths hot, they stoked each other's greed. Tugging off her panties, he took the lead, tempering his strength with tenderness while, with agonizing slowness, he brought them both to another mutual, soul-shattering climax.

Daylight waned as they reposed in each others' arms. As dusk slid into night, Clint carried her into the bedroom. Holding her body against his, he watched her succumb to sleep. It was only the distant roll of thunder that summoned him to his senses.

Tia. He'd made a promise to his daughter.

He looked down at Sonya's face. Tonight he'd forged a connection with this woman that went beyond physical intimacy, an unexpected and tenuous bond that, for the first time in many years, filled him with hope.

Guilt and desire engaged him in a relentless tug-of-war. With regret corroding his soul, he slipped out of her bed. He had responsibilities he couldn't ignore. He only hoped Sonya would understand. Perhaps she would if he could give her an explanation. Which he couldn't.

When Sonya awoke, in the middle of the night with thunder crashing overhead, only Rock's scent was left in the bed.

THE NEXT MORNING, Sonya reviewed the schedule for the photo shoot with Neil. Although it was only seven-thirty, the studio bustled with activity as technicians set up and tested the lighting, while artists placed the appropriate backdrops and props in the designated areas. They'd finish up the test shots today and finalize everything. Shooting would begin for real on Monday.

Neil shivered, overlapped the lapels of his blazer and anchored it in place with his arms across his chest. "It's like a deep freeze in here."

Because her internal temperature was as frigid as the air in the studio, Sonya shrugged. "It'll heat up soon enough, once the lights are turned on."

"Speaking of heat, how was your dinner with Rock last night?"

Her forced smile stretched her tight face. "Fine."

"Just...fine?"

She ticked off an item on her clipboard. "I don't want to talk about it, Neil."

"Something happened to upset you." Neil's eyes widened. "Did he force himself on you?"

"Force implies resistance." She tasted the bitter residue of her failed laugh. "Believe me, last night there was no resistance involved."

Neil lowered his voice. "Did he hurt you?"

Sonya's pen gouged the checklist. "Not in the physical sense." She looked at Neil, her best and only friend in Calgary, and sighed. He'd never betray her confidence. "Instead of me being the one to leave, he walked out while I slept."

Neil groaned. "Oh, sweetie. I'm so sorry."

"Don't be. I was a consenting adult. Granted, I hadn't planned on a one-night stand." She straightened her shoulders. "But you take the risk, you accept the consequences. It's over and done with."

"Is it?"

"Yes. I won't allow it to happen again."

Wisely, Neil said nothing.

"Can you double-check that the caterers will have lunch ready at twelve, sharp?"

"Yes, ma'am."

"And don't forget to inventory Cindy's film. What comes out of the studio has to match what came in."

"Gotcha."

When Rock strode into the studio, Sonya quelled the butterflies in her stomach and focused on the status report from the advertising department. Ignoring his heated gaze, she noted a discrepancy on the run date of one of the publications. Thankfully, as she'd instructed, Neil collared the cowboy and supervised the setup of the first shot.

Rock and Tiffany, a female model who was attired in a sparkling ball gown, posed under the spotlight, Rock dipping Tiffany back over his arm. The shot emphasized his denim-clad derriere and long legs, with tanned biceps bulging from the sleeves of a white T-shirt. The expression of sultry invitation on Tiffany's beautiful face left no doubt as to the attractiveness of the mysterious cowboy, whose Stetson shadowed the upper part of his face.

During the processing of the film, a crowd of tuxedo-clad dancers would be electronically added so that the final product would show the cowboy and his sophisticated escort at a formal ball. The caption underneath the billboard would read "Stand Out in a Crowd with Rocky Ridge Blue Jeans".

Cindy snapped a Polaroid, which Neil brought over for Sonya's approval.

"Perfect." She handed the photo back to him for safekeeping. "We'll get another couple of poses to choose from. Can you make sure you confiscate all the film and photos?"

As Sonya observed the session, she felt nothing inside. The ice encasing her heart froze out all emotion. Last night, she'd voluntarily given herself to the cowboy, without reservation. She'd surrendered herself to the seduction of pure passion and intimacy, something no one else had ever tempted her to do before. In return, she'd experienced a physical pleasure beyond her wildest dreams. But his nocturnal departure had mirrored those of her mother's endless cowboy parade. Sonya was in danger of falling into the same trap her mother had, a trap she'd successfully avoided for so long. A trap where one memorable night could lead to a lifetime of anguish. She was paying the price she hadn't anticipated and was unqualified to handle.

Heartache.

THE MORNING CRAWLED BY for Clint. The inactivity of
waiting, then holding a pose for an indeterminable
length of time, didn't strain his muscles so much as
his patience. Sonya wasn't giving him the proverbial
cold shoulder; she wouldn't let him close enough for
that. As he'd headed out the door the night before,
he'd considered leaving her a note, but then realized
there was nothing he could tell her to explain his actions. He'd expected her to be miffed, to demand an
explanation as to why he'd disappeared. He hadn't
expected her to act as though their intimacy hadn't
taken place at all.

He needed answers.

But she continued to avoid him. She kept herself at
a distance from the action, using Neil as her messen-
ger. Clint's frustration built, compounded by the fact
that, when he'd reached home the night before, the
baby-sitter had informed him Tia had fallen asleep,
disappointed at her father's absence. He'd apologized
to Tia over breakfast, but she still wasn't ready to forgive and forget. Females. You couldn't win, no matter
how hard you tried.

When they finally broke for lunch, Clint declined
Tiffany's blatant invitation to share a table with her.
Instead, he headed for Sonya's office. As he'd suspected, she was engrossed in her work, a half-eaten
sandwich on her desk.

Hamstrung by awkwardness, he strove to be casual. "Hi."

She stiffened, then spoke without looking up. "As
you can see, I'm busy right now."

Her iciness stung him. That had always been Kristin's weapon of choice, too. But Sonya was as different from Kristin as night was from day. Wasn't she?

He'd hoped they could at least be friends, that they'd be able to share a mutually satisfying physical relationship. Last night, he thought he'd discovered something more. Now he was afraid he'd only found in her what he'd wanted to see, that her coldness was not just skin-deep, but soul-deep. "About last night—"

"Yes." She flipped through a file on her desk. "Thank you for not disturbing me when you left. It was most considerate of you."

The chill in her voice sliced into Clint's heart. He should've known better than to think Sonya was anything but a cool and competent businesswoman. Look at the games she'd played with MacLeod; last night had only been a variation. It had meant more to him than it had to her.

At least he knew better than to delude himself further. He strove to keep his voice even. "Glad to have been of service." He whirled on his heel.

"Oh, cowboy."

He stopped and slowly turned to face her.

Her eyes were amber ice. "Tomorrow morning, I'll be driving down to the ranch with Neil. We'll see you at nine."

Knowing he had nothing to gain, but everything to lose, he flicked the brim of his Stetson. "Yes, ma'am." He stalked out of the room, his dignity barely intact.

9

THE COOL MORNING AIR slid through Sonya's hair as she and Neil cruised in a sporty convertible down the flat expanse of highway in southwestern Alberta. When they'd left Calgary, the mountains had appeared as jagged teeth on the bottom jaw of the horizon. Now an impressive backdrop of gray granite peaks rose from behind the green velvet folds of the foothills.

"Are we heading in the right direction?" She chanced a look at Neil, who was fighting the strong breeze to keep the map plastered against the passenger-side dashboard.

The road had dwindled to a narrow, two-lane blacktop, alternately bordered by large fields of golden wheat, wire-strung pastures and the odd stand of poplars.

Raising his designer sunglasses onto the top of his head, Neil wrestled with the map, his finger tracing an invisible line on the wildly flapping paper. "According to Rock's ink blot, his ranch should be coming up on the right shortly, give or take a hundred miles or so." He opened the glove box and shoved the wrinkled map inside.

At the thought of seeing Rock again, Sonya's stomach flip-flopped. "Thanks for coming with me."

"No sweat." He grinned. "Besides, I've already

marked it down on my 'famous and powerful people who can't refuse me a favor' list."

"Who else do you have on the list?"

"Oh, the odd box office star, an Olympic athlete or two and a dozen or so heads of state."

"Well, I'm flattered to be included in such exalted company."

"Stop! We just passed it!"

She slammed on the brakes, shoved the car into reverse and backed up. The ornate log entrance proclaimed Silver S Ranch. The transmission ground as she fumbled shifting gears.

"Nervous, sweetie?"

"No." She clenched the steering wheel. "I just don't want to be alone with him."

"Don't worry. I excel at playing third wheel."

During the dusty and rutted drive to the ranch buildings, Sonya was grateful for Neil's distracting chatter. She eased the convertible to a stop in front of a single-story log structure with a steep-pitched gable that soared like a mountain peak over the main entrance.

Rock detached himself from one of the thick log posts that supported the roof of the spacious veranda. In his faded blue jeans and white T-shirt, he exuded taut masculinity. A sensuous shiver ripped through her at the memory of that powerful body poised over her own, his strength tempered with tenderness.

Today, Sonya couldn't detect any warmth in the firm planes of his face. Not that it would prove anything if she had. She'd probably been just another notch on his bedpost.

"Good morning." His voice was measured, his greeting neutral, his gaze steady.

Once out of the car, Sonya removed her denim jacket and stretched her tense muscles. Belatedly, she realized the action caused her rose-colored tank top to outline her breasts in almost perfect detail. Her nipples pebbled under Rock's cursory glance.

As he turned his attention to Neil, she flushed and tossed her jacket in the car. If he could affect her with a simple look, what would happen in close proximity? If only she'd known, when she'd decided to succumb to passion, just how much a person could become a slave to her senses. She had no choice but to exorcize those emotions; she couldn't allow them to interfere with her job. In an effort to regain her composure, she reached into the back seat and retrieved her flat-topped, straw sun hat accented with a floral band.

"Nice hat," Rock drawled.

In defiance of the sarcasm in his voice, she raised her chin. "It'll be good protection."

A challenge flickered in the depths of his eyes. "From whom?"

From you. "From the sun."

Neil broke the tension. "Okay, guys. Let's start scouting."

Rock gestured toward a nearby corral. "The horses are saddled and ready to go."

Sonya regarded the animals with alarm. "It was nice of you to go to all that trouble, but we'll drive."

"Impossible. The terrain's too rugged for even a four-wheel drive, much less that half-baked dinky car." He cast a dubious look at their shorts and sandaled feet. "I should've told you what to wear, but I guess we'll have to make do."

Neil crossed his arms over his chest. "Forget it. You're not getting me up on one of those beasts."

"Fine. You stay here. While you scout the house and barn, I'll take Sonya on a tour of the ranch property."

Anxiety seized Sonya. "Neil."

Her assistant responded to the appeal in her voice with a helpless look. "I'm terrified of horses. I got thrown from one when I was a kid."

Her plan was going dangerously awry. "But...I don't know how to ride."

"Great." Rock sighed and rubbed his chin. "Then you'll have to ride double, with me."

"You have a double-seated saddle?"

A chuckle, rich with genuine amusement, relaxed the firm planes of Rock's face. "Sorry." He wagged his head. "Saddles don't come in two-seated models."

"So, where do we both sit?"

"I sit in the saddle." A wicked light gleamed in his eyes. "You sit in my lap."

Sonya's heart stuttered in horror. Just being near Rock taxed her diminished resistance, and her traitorous body already tingled at the thought of actual contact. She stared at him, unable to find a valid excuse for canceling the tour. She had a job to do.

ALL TOO CONSCIOUS of Sonya's rounded bottom tucked against his groin and the glory of his thighs embracing hers, Clint clenched his jaw and guided Apollo onto the well-worn trail to the upper pastures. Any other day, he'd be rejoicing in the magnificence of the world around him, drawing deep breaths of the summer scents carried on the pristine mountain breezes.

But today, Sonya's feminine perfume infiltrated his senses and, against his better judgment, focused his attention on the splendor of the woman he held in his arms. A bewitching and sensual woman who excelled within her complex world of corporate machination.

A world light-years from his own. Would he never learn? After being burned by his first experience in that world, he'd chosen a more simplified life-style, one that suited his and Tia's needs. Why had he fooled himself into thinking it would be any different this time? He'd been seduced by his own hormones, and although Sonya hadn't protested at the time, she obviously regretted their physical involvement. Yet his body continued to crave her, and he longed to feel her flesh on his, around his, to lose himself in her again.

But there was more than hormones at stake here; there was his heart. It was a no-win situation. So he stiffened his spine and his resolve, determined to ignore the temptation sitting in his lap.

They emerged into a clearing, at the base of a gentle emerald swell furred with evergreens and poplars. Clint reined Apollo to a stop. The rich, bubbling trill of a Western Meadowlark broke the silence.

Sonya's sigh wisped at the edge of his taut nerves. "It's so beautiful, so vibrant."

Clint never tired of the spectacular scenery, and the fact that she shared his awe of nature kindled an unexpected affinity between them. "It's a privilege to live here."

"Have you always been a rancher?"

It bothered him that such an innocent question required such a careful reply. "I've always spent a lot of time outdoors. Working in an office in a crowded city has never held any appeal for me. Ranching is hard work, but I love it."

"What happened, I mean why…" Her voice trailed off.

"Why was the bank about to foreclose on me?"

"Really, I don't mean to pry. It's none of my business."

He surveyed the distant fields of golden grain. "Over the past few years, a combination of market changes and natural disasters increased my debt load. A declining demand for beef gouged projected profits, and then I lost an entire herd to an unknown virus. Just when it looked like I had a chance to recover, we had a few unusually dry summers, driest weather in decades."

"I remember hearing something about that. It caused uncontrollable brush fires, right?"

"Yep. Had one here, just before harvest last year." He pointed at the golden squares edging the road, bordered by black fingers of scorched trees. "We managed to create a fire wall and stave off the worst of the damage. The cows and barns were insured, but the fields weren't."

He remembered the helplessness he'd felt, standing there, watching the acrid smoke turn his world black. He swallowed. "We were lucky to save the animals and buildings. But all my cash had been invested in the cattle. With supply down and demand up, the price of feed skyrocketed. I finally had to sell the herd, at a loss. Again. I could've handled one or two poor years, not four or five."

Sonya murmured in sympathy.

"Since my savings had been wiped out, I remortgaged the ranch to purchase new stock for the expanding organic beef market. It'll be a few months before they're ready for market. My money and credit were gone, and so was my hope—until I saw the notice of the audition in the paper. I figured it was worth a shot." He shrugged. "You know the rest."

She tipped back her head to look at him, and the swell of her breasts came into view. "You're really at the mercy of the weather, aren't you?"

Her lush lips and body provoked wild fantasies. "Mother Nature is a wonderful lady, but every now and then, just like most women, she likes to remind us who's in charge."

As soon as the words were out of his mouth, he realized his foot had jumped right in. Straightening, Sonya turned her ramrod back on him. "Sonya, I'm sorry. I didn't mean that the way it sounded."

"No, you're right. Since the other night, that's exactly how I've treated you." Her voice was low. "Like an employee."

Apollo shifted as he drew her around to face him, causing her hip to graze his groin. In reaction to the friction, blood pooled there. "It's my fault. I shouldn't have allowed things to get out of control."

A rueful smile curved her rose-tinted lips. "It takes two to tango, cowboy."

He brushed away a fly that landed on the collar of her jacket. "I never was much good at dancing."

Her gaze held his. "I always step on my partners' toes."

He bent his head to hers. "Maybe you need lessons."

"I can't commit to a long-term schedule."

"Then we'll take it one dance at a time."

Their lips entwined in a slow waltz, lush with promise. Clint dropped Apollo's reins and, cupping Sonya's behind, he lifted her around until she faced him. Tail swishing, Apollo lowered his head and began grazing.

When their brims collided, they tossed their hats aside. She peeled off her top to reveal a demure white morsel of lace. His arousal straining, he traced the swell of her breasts with his brown fingers, before slipping open the front clasp of her bra. When her breasts tumbled free, Clint palmed them and rubbed his thumbs over her erect nipples. "You have such a beautiful body."

Arching her back, she moaned her pleasure. His mouth closed over one perfect mound and his tongue laved its peak. Her hands tangled in his hair, before sliding down to tug his shirt off. The whisper of her fingers exploring his chest drove him to distraction.

Sonya unfastened her shorts and tried to push them down over the swell of her hips.

"Need some help?"

"Be right back." She slid to the ground and shucked her shorts, underwear and sandals.

Clint's breath caught at the sight of her, perfectly naked in the bright sunshine, her rose-tipped toes lost in the lush grass and wildflowers. "Don't move." He reached behind the saddle and untied his bedroll.

Seconds later, they lay on the makeshift bed. Sonya's clever fingers quickly freed him and stroked his hardened shaft. Cradling her face in his hands, Clint reclaimed her lips as their bodies strained toward one another, each greedy touch leading to another.

His breathing ragged, he poised himself over her. She clutched his hips, her demanding hands and moans of desire revealing her desperate need. On the brink of losing control, he complied and, inch by torturous inch, slid into her. Her hot, slick heat closed around him, a perfect fit. She linked her arms around his neck and urged him to increase their rhythm. Clint obeyed, rejoicing in the sensation of her breasts grazing his chest. She climaxed, crying his name, and he emptied himself into her shuddering core.

Sonya slumped against Rock's solid frame, her senses slowly tumbling back to earth. Had she really just made love in the middle of a meadow? She opened her eyes. Yep. She was buck naked, in the arms of an almost nude and heart-stoppingly attractive cowboy.

Total decadence.

Talk about losing control! She basked in the residue of their wild pleasure. For some reason, her good intentions always dissolved in Rock's presence. The logical part of her knew the piper would eventually have to be paid, but her wicked side rejoiced when Rock hugged her closer in his arms.

Propped on an elbow, Clint watched Sonya doze in the late-morning sun. Why did she drive herself so relentlessly? He had no doubt MacLeod set impossibly high standards for his staff, but he also suspected Sonya's expectations of herself were even more stringent. Someday her overachieving personality would exact a heavy toll, and he wouldn't be there to protect her. He'd love to be her champion, but Sonya's fierce independence would never allow her to accept that. A keen sense of loss sliced through his sensual contentment.

He stroked a wildflower down the side of Sonya's face. She raised a listless hand and wiped it away, but he repeated the action. Her drowsy lids opened, revealing guileless golden eyes. A sensual smile spread to her kiss-plumped lips. He continued skimming the bloom over the pale skin of her shoulder, over the swell of her breast, down the contours of her stomach and hip.

She stretched like a cat and positively purred. "Again?"

He lay the rose in the valley between her breasts, then bent down and brushed her lips with his own. He grinned. "And again. But unless we get you covered up, all that lovely skin is going to glow like a prairie sunset tonight."

"Mmm. I'd like it to glow for some other reason." She stroked his face with her fingers.

The full impact of the situation hit him. How could he tell her that nights were off-limits, without explaining why? Retreating from her touch, he handed over her discarded clothes and she began to dress.

After the disruption and upheaval of his final year with Kristin, he'd made a personal vow to set a good example for his daughter. And that didn't include abandoning her overnight with a baby-sitter so he could find sexual satisfaction, or bringing home a string of temporary lovers. If and when he fell in love with the right kind of woman who could be a suitable mother to Tia, he would relax that rule.

Regrettably, Sonya couldn't be that woman.

He pulled on his T-shirt. "We'd better finish the tour and get back to the ranch."

"Rock?" She touched his arm. "Is everything all right?"

"Everything's fine." The lie added weight to his increasing burden of guilt. "I've got lunch waiting for us in the fridge."

Sonya checked her watch. "Oh my God, poor Neil will be frantic."

Clint tucked the rose behind her ear and dropped a light kiss on her lips. "I'll grab Apollo while you get dressed." The tenuous relationship between him and Sonya was too unpredictable for him to reveal Tia's existence and the sordid events surrounding Kristin's death. As he'd told her, they'd take it one dance at a time.

Admiring Sonya's shapely legs and the curve of her hips, he helped Sonya mount Apollo. He was in the process of swinging up behind her when a couple of horses burst into the clearing.

"Daddy!"

CLINT LOWERED HIS LEG to the ground, hoping it was all just a bad dream. But when he looked up, Tia and Katie, their faces avid with curiosity, pulled up beside him.

"Hi, Mr. Silver." Katie's braids bounced as she turned her head to eye Sonya.

He smiled fondly at his daughter's best friend. "Hi, Katie."

He took a quick look at Sonya and his heart sank at the shock etched on her face.

Tia vaulted off Zork and threw her arms around his waist. Clint hugged her, chucked her under the chin and yanked a dangling red curl. "Where are you off to in such a hurry?"

Tia gestured to her backpack. "We're goin' up to Paradise Lake for lunch." Mischief sparkled from her dark blue eyes. "We were kinda havin' a race up the slope." She looked to Katie for support.

"Yeah," Katie chimed. "And I was winning."

"But I was catching up," Tia insisted.

"Racing? On a warm day like this?" Clint touched a finger to the tip of her freckled nose. "Poor old Zork isn't as young as he used to be."

Tia shifted her attention to Sonya, who was plucking the petals from the wilting rose. "Who's she?"

"Remember I told you I was going to be renting the ranch to some people from Calgary?"

Tia nodded. "That's why you sent me over to Katie's. 'Cause it isn't 'propriate for children to be around."

"That's right, pumpkin." Clint appealed to Sonya with his eyes. "Ms. Duncan is in charge of the project and I'm giving her a tour."

"Tia, Katie, this is Ms. Duncan." He turned to Sonya. "This is my daughter, Tia, and her friend, Katie."

Sonya gave the girls a tentative smile. "Hi."

"Hi." Tia eyed Sonya. "Where's her horse?"

"I don't know how to ride." Sonya's voice was defensive.

Tia's eyes widened. "You don't?"

"Ms. Duncan is from Toronto," Clint explained.

"Wow!" Tia regarded Sonya with interest. "That's where my favorite band, the Bay Street Boyz, are from."

Sonya nodded. "They're a nice bunch of guys."

Tia's jaw dropped. "You know them?"

"My, uh, company designed the cover for their latest compact disc."

"Ms. Duncan and I have to get back to work." Clint

scooped up Tia's hat, set it on her head and adjusted the leather cord under her chin. "Do you have your sunscreen with you?"

Tia, her eyes glued on Sonya, gave him an absent nod.

His worst fears were realized at the look of outright awe and respect on the preteens' faces. He wouldn't allow Tia to become a victim of the same industry that had claimed her mother. "Go have your lunch. I'll see you at supper."

With lithe grace, Tia climbed back up on Zork and tugged on the reins to raise the grazing animal's head.

Sonya waved her fingers at the girls.

"Bye, Ms. Duncan," they chorused, and urged their mounts into a trot. Clint watched them ride off, delaying the moment when he'd have to turn and face Sonya.

"You've got some major explanations to make, *Mr. Silver*."

It was time to employ damage control.

Striving for a casual grin, he swung around and looked up at Sonya. "That was close."

She shot him a glance, her eyes slitted beneath the brim of her straw hat. *"That was close?"* She planted her fists on her thighs. "Your daughter and her friend, a couple of prepubescent girls, almost caught us frolicking in the meadow together—nude—and all you can say is that was close?" Chest heaving, Sonya slid off Apollo to confront him, face-to-face. "Do you have any idea how traumatic that could have been for them?"

Once again he'd allowed his hormones to cloud his common sense. Guilt chased through him, spurring his anger. He leveled a stare at Sonya, his words bullets of indignation. "Do you think I knew the two girls would be here? What the hell kind of father do you think I am?"

"How should I know? I had no idea you even were a father!" Sonya's eyes blazed molten gold. "Why the hell didn't you tell me?"

They glared at each other in simultaneous outrage. Sonya looked like a fierce golden cougar, ready to attack.

Clint shoved his Stetson back on his head. "Because I didn't want you to meet my daughter."

Shock overrode the anger on Sonya's face. "Why?"

Torn between his desire to protect Tia and his need to preserve the fragile bond he'd established with Sonya, Clint said nothing.

"I see." The tension lines around her mouth whitened. "I'm okay when it comes to a quick tumble in the meadow, but I'm not good enough to meet your daughter."

Damn! "That's not what this is about."

"Isn't it? I want you to know I'm not the kind of woman who flaunts her sexual encounters in front of an impressionable young girl." Sonya's voice trembled with emotion. "And I'm not interested in a man who would do that to his daughter."

Stunned by the self-disgust in her voice, Clint found the last of his anger ebbing away. Something awful must have happened in Sonya's past for her to react like this. Whatever it was, he had the feeling it would explain the coldness of her behavior yesterday.

He wanted to help her, yet in doing so, he would become more emotionally involved with her. It was a danger he didn't take lightly, neither for himself or Tia, since a permanent relationship between him and Sonya was an impossibility. But he had little choice, as tendrils of feelings for her had already taken root in his heart. There was no going back.

Clint sighed. "You've got it all wrong. Tia is the most important thing in my life. I've raised her the best I could, and personally, I think I've done a damn good job."

"Oh, my God." Sonya's eyes widened. "*She's* the one you're protecting!"

Clint nodded. "That's right."

Aghast at her emotional outburst, Sonya stared at Rock. Her anger withered like the wildflower still clasped in her hand. "And she's the reason you left the other night."

"I'm sorry, Sonya. It was impossible to explain why."

He hadn't been condemning her for her wanton behavior, he'd been protecting Tia. Admiration of his deep love for his daughter was followed by Sonya's mortification at the knowledge that she herself was a participant in the same scenario for which she'd denounced her mother. Except she'd switched roles. Now she was the temporary lover who had no intention of a long-term commitment.

Shame from the humiliating memories writhed within her and infused her heart with guilt. Her own course of action lay clear. Sonya drew a fortifying breath and turned her face up to Rock. "We're in an impossible situation."

He took her hand. "Look, we both know the time we have together is short, but we're two consenting adults. And I've already made arrangements so Tia won't be anywhere near the ranch when you and your crew arrive."

Both she and her mother had paid too high a price for Sonya to ignore the lesson from the past. Like the wild rose dying in her hand, her brief blooming had been spectacular. She couldn't cultivate her own pleasure at Tia's expense. Grief seized the fragile petals of her emotion and crushed them. Her eyes filled with tears. "You don't understand. Tia changes everything."

He stiffened, then dropped her hand. "Unfortunately, I do understand. Some women can't accept the responsibility of children."

"I know. My mother was one of them." Sonya swallowed the sorrow clogging her throat. "I owe you an explanation."

Rock's hands framed her face, his green eyes dark with concern. With a gentle sweep of his thumb, he wiped away an errant tear. "You don't owe me a thing."

The tenderness in his touch caused fresh tears to spring into her eyes. "No, it's past time I told you." She squared her shoulders, thankful for the compassion she'd found in him. "I told you a little bit about my childhood."

He nodded. "You don't have a father, your mother died when you were eleven and you lived with your grandmother for six years."

This was the difficult part. By sharing her pain with him, she would be giving him a piece of her heart. Yet if she withheld the information, he'd believe her heartless. Despite that they had no future, it was important she retain his respect. "My mother met my father during the Calgary Stampede. He was a rodeo cowboy and she was a stage performer. Mom said it was love at first sight."

She blinked and Rock stroked the side of her face in encouragement.

"On the final night of the Stampede, they made love. My father gave her his championship rodeo buckle and promised to return for her in a month."

Clint sighed. "A silver buckle designed like a lariat."

"Yes. She wore it on a chain around her neck until the day she died." Sonya bit her lip. "She never doubted he'd come back."

"Did he?"

"No. She never saw or heard from him again." Sonya lowered her eyes and focused on the pull of the T-shirt across Rock's broad chest. "She started drinking and accepted gigs in any and all country-and-western bars, hoping to find him. The cowboys learned that if they pretended to know my father, they could take advantage of her." She swallowed. "And they did."

Rock folded her in his arms. "Did any of them ever touch you?"

"One night, one of them lurched into my room and tried to grope me in the dark. I screamed and grabbed my baseball bat. Luckily, he was too drunk to react quickly. I got in a couple of good wallops before my mother threw him out." Sonya's lips curled at the memory. "For two years in a row, I had the highest hitting average in the league. Anyway, after that night, Mom promised she'd stop drinking, but she couldn't. Sometimes she'd last a few days, but she always broke her promises. So I always locked my door when she…entertained."

"Your mother must have been a very lonely woman."

The tender growl of his voice comforted her. A couple of tears dripped onto his shirt. "Yes," she whispered into his neck.

Clint palmed her chin and raised her head so he could look directly into her eyes. "You're nothing like your mother."

"I've always lived with the fear that I might be," she admitted. "That's why my career is so important to me."

He nodded. "It proves you have control over your life."

"I'm not so sure anymore." She gestured at Apollo, then the meadow. "I've never done things like this before."

"Me either." He grinned. "I think it could easily become a habit."

"That's what I'm afraid of."

His arms tightened around her as he kissed the top of her head. "I'm glad you decided you could confide in me."

"I knew you'd agree."

"About what?"

She swallowed past the lump constricting her throat. "Us."

He shook his head. "I'm not sure I follow you."

A keen sense of loss pierced her heart. Tears clouding her eyes, she reached up and touched his cheek. "This was our last dance."

10

THE EARLY MORNING SUN winked off the walls of windows on apartment building complexes as Clint drove through the outskirts of Calgary. He steered the dusty pickup around a curve on the deserted ramp of the expressway and was confronted by a giant billboard advertising Rocky Ridge blue jeans. Applying the brakes, he slowed down and stared at the sign. Sonya had been right; in the midst of the tuxedoed crowd, the jeans stood out. The lady was a genius. No wonder MacLeod was afraid of her.

He hadn't had an opportunity to speak to her alone since that afternoon at the ranch two weeks ago. Ever since, he'd put in long days in the studio, and when Sonya was there, half a dozen bodies surrounded her. Otherwise, she was tied up in meetings. He missed her. Missed the entrancing way she had touched him, the blatant sensuality that gleamed from her eyes when she gave herself up to pure feeling, her incredible determination and her unexpected vulnerability. No other woman had ever had such an impact on him.

The success of the campaign was great for Sonya and great for his financial well-being, but it only increased the impossibility of their ever being together. She would obtain her promotion and go back to her world, while he remained in his. It was futile to long for what couldn't be. The solution was to work as hard as he could in order to keep his mind off Sonya and lessen the term of his torture.

As he neared the office complex that housed Zenith Communications' offices, he pulled the peak of his baseball cap lower and adjusted the dusty sun visor. Since the first newspaper ads had appeared a week ago, he'd left his Stetson in the studio. Each day, the horde of reporters, surrounding the entrances to the building grew larger. Any man entering the place with a Stetson was swarmed. Only the recent presence of burly security guards kept the media vultures off the twenty-first floor.

Despite the early hour, the parking garage was packed with vehicles sporting the gaudy logos of both local and national media. Wearing a baggy one-piece coverall that concealed his jeans and T-shirt, Clint strolled toward a service elevator. A couple of eager reporters broke away from the crush encircling the main elevators and accosted him.

"Excuse me." A thin, gangly man with an impossibly deep voice and a tape recorder under his arm tugged at Clint's elbow and shoved a microphone in front of his face. "Five hundred dollars is yours if you can tell me who Rock is."

"Hey, that's small potatoes. I'll give you a thousand!" A balding middle-aged man in a wrinkled gray suit shoved his card at Clint. "Call me, anytime."

Clint pulled a handkerchief from his pocket and faked a coughing fit. As he hawked noisily into the white cloth, the reporters turned away in disgust. Shaking his head, Clint used his utilitarian lunch pail to force his way through the crowd. He shoved the handkerchief and the card into a hip pocket. He had to talk to Sonya about this; they couldn't take a chance on anyone finding out the location of his ranch.

When the elevator stopped on the twenty-first floor, the security guards inspected the identification badge that proclaimed him to be Thomas Sparks, a janitor, and waved him on.

Sonya and Neil were huddled over her desk, coffee mugs at their elbows. Sonya looked up, a broad smile on her face. "Rock, have you seen this?"

Neil held up a newspaper. "We made the front page of today's *Calgary Herald*."

"You can't buy this kind of publicity," Sonya enthused. "You were right. The media's really grabbed ahold of the idea."

Clint read the headline "Who Is Rock, the Mysterious Model Cowboy?". The photo showed a smiling Harvey Wilson standing in the middle of a store packed with people. Clint's stomach tightened. "What does the article say?"

"It talks about the phenomenal increase in sales for Rocky Ridge blue jeans and how the customers are demanding to know who the mysterious cowboy is." Sonya held out her hand. "Congratulations, Rock."

The warmth of her hand delivered a chilled arrow of regret directly to his heart. "The credit's all yours. You're the creative genius behind the whole thing. I just followed orders."

She disengaged her hand from his. "Yes, but it was your idea in the first place."

"Enough, already." Neil jabbed his finger into his open mouth and pretended to gag. "I'm sure there's a seat for both of you on the modesty train."

Clint managed a smile. "Thanks, Neil. Would you mind if I have a moment alone with Sonya?"

Neil's speculative glance slid from him to Sonya. "It would be my pleasure. Take your time." He grinned. "I'll make sure things are ready in the studio."

Dark shadows smudged Sonya's eyes. Concern flooding him, Clint sat down. "How are you?"

"Fine." She twirled a pen in her fingers. "What's up?"

Behind her smile, he saw the trepidation evident by her rigid posture. She still wanted him, as much as he wanted her, and if he caressed the curve of her cheek or touched his lips to hers, she'd be putty in his hands. They both knew that, but it couldn't move the mountain of constraint between them. He hunched forward. "I'm getting worried. I just had two reporters outbidding each other on information about the identity of the Rocky Ridge man."

A smile of satisfaction lit her face. "I think we may have unleashed a monster. Good thing this is the last day for the studio shoot."

"Are you sure your people can be trusted?"

"Absolutely." Her direct gaze took the edge off his uneasiness. "I handpicked them myself. Besides, most of them know next to nothing about you, anyway." She looked away. "Even me."

He sighed. "You can't reveal what you don't know."

"In other words, you don't trust me."

The truth hit home. As much as he desired her body and admired her mind, he couldn't completely trust her. "I'm sorry, Sonya."

"I prefer to hear the truth."

The gulf between them widened. Clint strove to get back to the subject at hand. "What about security at the ranch?"

"We should be okay. I've contracted a private film crew from Toronto. They're flying in Wednesday with their own equipment and will go directly to the ranch, so the local media won't even be aware of it. Since everyone will be housed on site, it'll cut down on the usual coming and going."

Clint drummed his fingers on her desk. "If there's a huge convoy all arriving at once, my neighbors will be sure to notice."

"Don't worry, our schedule has all the precision of a military plan." Her pen tapped her clipboard. "The arrival of vehicles and equipment will be staggered over a number of days."

"Where will you be staying?"

She doodled on a piece of scrap paper. "Neil and I will bunk in one of the motor homes."

Despite the firmness in her statement, Clint found the thought of being near her without being able to touch her torturous. His base, male need for her drove him to press her on the issue. "Would I be a total hypocrite if I suggested the ranch house would be a whole lot more comfortable?"

Her gaze was clear and direct. "No. But it would be a lot more complicated. Right now, I need to keep my life as uncomplicated as possible, so I can concentrate on the Rocky Ridge campaign."

He admired her strength, although he detested its implications. "Let me know if you change your mind."

"Rock?"

He turned.

"I wish I could give you a different answer." Her eyes, filled with regret, spoke to him louder than her words.

"So do I."

EARLY WEDNESDAY MORNING, Sonya pulled the mammoth motor home into the yard in front of Rock's ranch house, shut off the engine and leaned her forehead against the steering wheel. In order to avoid the rain predicted for late morning, she'd left at the crack of dawn. Her arms ached from the stress of trying to restrain the metal beast from leaping onto the shoulder of the road. Her heart ached at the thought of never being held in Rock's arms again.

Squaring her shoulders, she knocked on the front door. Since she'd severed her physical relationship with Rock, she'd made sure she hadn't spent any time alone with him. But distance and time hadn't proved to be allies. Two and half weeks later, her desire for him was stronger than ever. She'd just have to ignore it and eventually the craving would wane. Wouldn't it?

But she wasn't being paid to yearn. She had a job to do. When no one answered the door, she walked in. The sound of country-and-western music drew her toward the kitchen area. As she passed through the spacious living area, with its honeyed log walls and floor-to-ceiling fieldstone fireplace, the warmth of the casual decor seeped into her bones. That was the first thing she'd noticed about Rock's home when she'd toured it two weeks ago: an appealing ambience of simplicity. Neil had termed it "early prairie retrograde," but the house's homespun personality reminded her of the simple two-bedroom bungalow that her grandmother had lovingly decorated with her own handcrafted creations. Items that weren't made to make an impression, but to provide warmth and comfort.

An enticing aroma of percolating coffee assailed her nostrils as she entered the buttercup-yellow kitchen. Tia stood at the stove, vigorously stirring a skillet of scrambled eggs, while bacon sizzled in a second skillet. Sonya's stomach rumbled. The piece of toast she'd washed down a couple of hours ago had dissipated and left her with a raging appetite.

"Hi, Tia."

The lithe preteen turned, shot her a startled glance, then smiled. "Hi, Ms. Duncan."

Tia's easy acceptance of her arrival endeared her to Sonya. The young girl's budding maturity reminded Sonya of another young girl who'd struggled to undertake the burden of caring for an incapacitated parent. Obviously, Rock's daughter was fortunate to have at least one nurturing parent. "Call me Sonya."

"Okay...Sonya." Her deep blue eyes shone with gratitude at the privilege of being considered an equal. "Would you like some coffee?"

"Thanks. I'd love some." Sonya smiled in appreciation. "Since you're busy, just tell me where the mugs are and I'll get it myself."

After pouring herself a mug of the aromatic brew, Sonya sat at the rough-hewn pine table, where two places had been set. The room's combination of aged pine and yellow paint, along with the flower-sprinkled calico curtains, conveyed a lighthearted welcome.

Tia put a cover on the skillet of eggs, placed it on a back burner and turned down the heat under the bacon before setting a matching place mat and cutlery in front of Sonya.

"Daddy should be back in a few minutes." She pushed a red-gold curl over her shoulder.

"Great. That'll give us some time for girl talk." Rock's daughter fascinated her. Although she didn't physically resemble her father, Tia's smile and calm assurance were pure Rock, which was all the more reason Sonya shouldn't take any chance on coming between the two. As much as she longed to pump the girl about her father, she knew it would be a mistake. Instead, she took a long sip of coffee, desperately searching her mind for a safe topic of conversation. "How old are you, Tia?"

"Almost eleven."

The same age she'd been when her mother had died. "You're very mature for your age."

"Do you think I'm old enough to get my ears pierced?"

Dangerous question. "What does your father think?"

Tia rolled her eyes. "He says I can get them pierced when I'm fifty."

Sonya laughed and leaned toward Tia. "Why doesn't that surprise me? What does your mother say?"

Tia's face clouded. "My mother died when I was three."

Aghast, Sonya found her heart going out to the girl. That's what Rock had meant when he'd said he didn't have a wife. "I'm sorry. You must miss her."

Tia shook her head. "I don't really remember her, and Daddy doesn't like to talk about her."

If he found it that difficult to talk about his ex-wife

to his own daughter, he must have loved her deeply. Maybe that's why he'd never remarried—no other woman could measure up. The thought speared Sonya's heart. "I see."

"Katie's twelve next month, and she's getting her ears pierced for her birthday."

"Maybe your father will change his mind."

Tia sighed. "I don't think so. He doesn't like talking about girl stuff at all. He won't let me wear any makeup, either."

"Are girls wearing makeup at your age?" The thought shocked Sonya.

The girl nodded, then whispered, "Some of them even have boyfriends."

Children were growing up so fast these days. No wonder Rock was so protective.

"I don't want a boyfriend, though." Tia picked at the fringe of her place mat. "I just want to look cool and wear cool clothes like the girls in the magazines Katie has."

Sonya nodded. She remembered wanting the affirmation of looking pretty at Tia's age, too; but Rock's daughter wasn't merely pretty, she was stunning. "You know, the clothes those girls model don't belong to them, and they don't look so glamorous in real life. Most of the time, they hang out in jeans and shirts, just like you."

"Really?" Tia's eyes widened. "How do you know?"

"My company hires girls like them for magazine ads and commercials."

Sipping from a glass of orange juice, Tia digested the information. "In Toronto, right?"

"Have you been there?"

"No. Dad doesn't like cities much."

It was apparent the girl's exposure beyond the ranch had been limited. Without a mother to guide her, and with Rock's reluctance to discuss girl stuff, the poor thing would be a tomboy for the rest of her life. Maybe Sonya could help Tia explore her feminine side. "As a matter of fact, we've just opened an office in Calgary. In the next couple of months, we'll be putting together a talent bank."

Tia leaned forward. "What's that?"

"We keep photos on file of people who are interested in modeling or acting."

"Can anyone do it?"

"Sure." Sonya took a fortifying sip of coffee. "We're always looking for fresh faces. Would you be interested in being a model, Tia?"

"No!" Rock strode into the room, the door slamming behind him. "It's completely out of the question for my daughter to be a model."

"Daddy," Tia implored, "I want to."

"I'm sorry, sweetheart." Rock raked Sonya with a contemptuous glare, then turned back to his daughter. "The answer is no."

Tia pushed out her lower lip and locked her arms across her chest. "I'm old enough to make up my own mind."

Her father sighed. "Have you finished packing, Tia?"

"No."

"Why don't you go finish that?" His voice softened. "In a few minutes, I'll call you for breakfast."

Tia stomped out of the room. Rock turned his back to Sonya and poured himself some coffee; the hand holding the carafe trembled slightly. "You're early," he accused.

Shocked by the intensity of Rock's reaction, Sonya babbled, "I wanted to get here before the rainstorm hits. With the wind as strong as it is, I was lucky to make it. The film crew will be arriving late this afternoon and Neil will drive another motor home down tomorrow."

Rock faced her with somber eyes, grim lines etched around his mouth. "So we start shooting the day after tomorrow?" His words were clipped.

Why was he so angry? Did it have something to do with his need to protect his daughter? Or was he angry because Sonya wouldn't sleep with him anymore? His disapproval stung, more than she wanted it to. She stood and faced him. "Look, I'm sorry if I upset you. I just thought Tia might enjoy modeling. And she certainly has what it takes."

"Oh, what exactly does it take?" The edge in Rock's voice caused gooseflesh to prickle her skin.

Despite a warning tremor, she replied, "Good bone structure, plus healthy skin and hair."

"Anything else?"

Sonya licked her dry lips. "To make it to the top, a model also has to have a burning desire to succeed."

"A desire so great she's willing to sacrifice everything else to achieve it," he growled.

Was he talking about Tia or her? "Within reason, yes."

He moved closer, his heat enveloping her. "Not everyone is capable of balancing reason with desire."

Sonya fought the overwhelming urge to surrender her body to his. She craved the strength of his arms, the gentleness of his fingertips caressing her skin, the heat of their bodies moving as one, the special magic that propelled them beyond mere reality. But she couldn't indulge herself. She raised her chin. "Surely that's up to the individual to decide."

"Right now, I make the decisions for Tia." Rock's intense gaze speared Sonya in place. "My daughter isn't going to live her life with one eye on the mirror, desperate to please others with her looks. She's going to use her brains to make a living."

"Why can't she use both her reason and her desire?"

Shadows of regret darkened Rock's eyes as he stared into hers. "It's been my experience that one usually gets sacrificed for the other."

Stunned by Rock's pain, Sonya stood dumbly as she watched him move to the stove to serve breakfast. She'd been so wrapped up in her own self-righteousness, she hadn't looked beyond her pain to his own. Had she contributed to the anguish she'd witnessed in his eyes? He had enough troubles without her adding to them. She ached to comfort him, but even if she did, all she could offer was a short-term solution. He and Tia deserved much more than that.

"CUT!" Myles, the director, a slender man with a trim goatee, leaned over and spoke to the camera operator.

The first assistant, her peroxided hair teased to an impossible height, called out, "Take five, but hold positions, please."

Clint stepped back from the midnight gelding and rolled his shoulders to ease the strain in his neck. Tiffany, resplendent in a white filmy gown and wide-brimmed hat, remained perched on top of the horse.

While Myles conferred with his assistant, Sonya

spoke with one of the technicians who'd approached her. Over the past few days, Clint had observed the easy camaraderie that existed between her and her staff. Sonya tended to listen more than talk, focusing her full attention on each person, whether it be the most junior of assistants or the most senior technician. In return, their actions and gestures demonstrated their respect for her.

It was obvious she loved her job and the people who worked with her. Feelings of pride and regret warred within Clint. Even if she cared for him the way he did for her, he could never ask her to give up her work. It was a part of her, in the same way the ranch was a part of him. He had to accept that reality, as much as he wished it could be different.

A female assistant in a skimpy tank top and denim shorts ran over and offered both him and Tiffany bottles of cold spring water. Clint accepted his with a smile, then turned around, his eyes connecting with Sonya's sunglasses. Since she was now alone, he waved her over, admiring the smooth motion of her hips as she walked and the mouthwatering length of her tanned legs.

He hadn't had a chance to apologize to her since the confrontation over Tia in the kitchen the other day. Together Sonya and Neil bore the burden of coordinating the massive effort of people and resources that were involved in the production process. Clint respected her cool competence and the way she provided quick solutions to each problem. If only an easy remedy existed for their personal situation.

"What's the problem?" The heat of the sun heightened the effect of her perfume, evoking memories of the day in the meadow, when her scent had surrounded him, lusty and sweet.

He lowered his voice. "I want to apologize for my behavior over Tia. You couldn't have known how strongly I feel about the modeling industry."

"I know you're only doing this to save your ranch." She gestured toward the golden fields and the majestic mountains towering into the vast blue of the sky. "And I've come to appreciate why you're so unwilling to lose it."

Before she asked the next obvious question, he changed the subject. "So, how much longer before we're done?"

"Can't take the heat, cowboy?" Her voice was light, teasing, yet he detected a hint of compassion behind it.

"You'd be surprised how much I can endure."

She must have caught his double meaning, because she shifted her weight and consulted her clipboard. "I think Myles wants another couple of shots of this, then we break for lunch. After that, there're a couple of hours free before we shoot the picnic scene."

Yearning to cool off, he leaned forward and pulled her sunglasses down the bridge of her nose. "Care for a swim?"

"Where?"

Visions of skinny-dipping with her tantalized his mind. "Paradise Lake."

"I don't have a bathing suit with me."

He grinned. "Perfect."

She hesitated and his anticipation soared. When she shook her head, hope took a nosedive.

"I can't. I've got a thousand and one details to go over."

The click and whir of a camera startled him. Heart thumping, he swung around to see the continuity girl taking his photo, to ensure the next shot matched with the last one. She smiled and shielded the developing film from the sun. Then the wardrobe lady moved in and held out a clean shirt for Clint. It was a duplicate of the one he was wearing.

"Sweat stains," she said.

Clint gave her an exaggerated groan. "This is the third shirt I've put on this morning. How many of these do you have?"

"A couple of dozen."

He shrugged and started to unbutton his shirt. "Believe it or not, real cowboys do sweat."

"Most of the time, people want things to be the way they imagine them to be, not the way they really are." Sonya, who had stepped back and slipped her sunglasses back up, gave him a wry smile. "So in television commercials, cowboys don't sweat."

Clint wished he could see her eyes. "That's the danger of illusions—once you start fooling yourself, you can't stop."

"Sometimes reality is hard to accept."

He'd learned that lesson the hard way. "You can't change reality, only your response to it."

"What do you mean?"

He'd mulled over the words innumerable times since Kristin's death. Even though his culpability prevented him from taking that advice, maybe he could help Sonya release the burden of her mother's legacy. "Don't live your life looking backward. Let go of the past. Face toward the future, but live in the present."

Her brow furrowed. "I'm living life exactly as I want."

"Are you?"

"Take your positions!" the nasal voice of the first assistant bellowed. "Quiet on the set."

As she hurried back to her observation spot, Sonya's mind whirled with the implications of Rock's remark. Nothing could change the reality of her grim childhood; she'd coped with it the best she'd been able. Of course, those circumstances had influenced the subsequent choices she'd made. Since she'd witnessed the destructiveness of instability, she'd decided to concentrate her efforts on her career, while other young women had sought love and family. Her bleak reality had actually spawned her success.

Was Rock suggesting she let go of the past so she'd change her mind and sleep with him? She was living in the present—her major responsibility was to see to the success of the Rocky Ridge campaign. As for the future, her job demanded she plan weeks, if not months, in advance. What Rock had said didn't make sense. Still, there'd been a depth of sincerity and emotion in his voice that spoke of a deep, personal battle. Maybe it had something to do with his wife's death. Maybe he had to let go of his past, too.

A few hours later, Sonya watched Rock reclining in the hot sun, Tiffany sitting at his side. A gingham quilt, picnic basket, lunch for two, a bottle of wine and wineglasses completed the scenario. The action called for them to clink glasses, then Tiffany would bend over and kiss Rock. It was the focal shot for the commercial entitled "Rocky Ridge High."

For the eighth time, Tiffany leaned over and kissed Rock, and for the eighth time, jealousy spiked Sonya's heart. It was ridiculous, of course, even pathetic, but each time their lips touched, her hurt deepened.

When Rock and Tiffany shared a private joke, the pain became unbearable. Maybe Tiffany was the type of woman who wouldn't think twice about having a fling with a totally unsuitable and rugged cowboy. Maybe she wouldn't worry about the repercussions on an impressionable ten-year-old. Maybe Rock would spend the whole night with her.

And what business was it of Sonya's? She'd told Rock that a fling with him, as tempting as it might be, was impossible, a long-term relationship an even greater impossibility. She scowled. Of course, Rock chose that exact moment to stand up, stretch his magnificent physique and walk over to her.

His gaze explored her from head to foot. "Why are you so hot and bothered?"

She chafed under his gaze. "Oh, I don't know. Maybe standing for hours in the hot sun might have something to do with it."

"We could have gone swimming."

She wiped the sweat from her forehead. "You know that wouldn't have been a good idea."

"I think it would have been just what we needed." He waggled his eyebrows in a suggestive manner.

"Right. I suppose I would've been a great warm-up for Tiffany."

He gestured toward the set and grinned. "Just doing my job."

Sonya bared her teeth. "Nice to see you enjoying it so much."

"You're jealous."

"Hardly."

"Liar."

He winked and she tossed her head. If he thought for one moment that she was affected by Tiffany kissing him, he was dead...right.

Because she loved him.

He waited and she tensed her heart. If he thought
for one moment the ratio was affected by telling her
leg limp, he was dead. Right.

Because she loved him.

11

THE SMELL OF sizzling steak spitting on the grill
drifted on the warm evening breeze. From his vantage point on the veranda, Clint surveyed the temporary encampment that had sprung up in his yard.
Sonya's world had invaded his. It was organized
chaos, with cables and hoses running from motor
homes to his barns, moving trucks regurgitating their
loads of equipment and the odd lawn chair sagging
under the weight of an embracing couple.

At Clint's suggestion, the former army cook hired
by Zenith Communications had set up the half-barrel
barbecue pits that were kept stored in the barn for the
Silver S's annual neighborhood barbecue. Scattered
groups of technicians and production assistants
sprawled on the grass or lounged at the picnic tables,
beers in hand. A couple of portable compact disc
players blasted the latest rock and country music. A
few of the less frenzied personalities lolled on the veranda, their feet propped up on the sturdy log rail. A
bellow of laughter from the burly and gregarious
cook rumbled above the hum of crickets and the distant mooing of cattle.

Clint drew on the bottle of ice-chilled beer, enjoying the sensation of the cold beverage spreading
through his body. After sluicing off his own dust and
perspiration, he'd offered the ranch's two showers to

supplement those in the motor homes. He hadn't seen Sonya since they'd returned from the picnic shoot. Being so close to her day after day was taking its toll. If he wasn't careful, his frustration level would spiral out of control. He needed to relax. Taking Apollo for a ride in the foothills would revitalize his spirit; the wind would blow all his worries away.

A warm body brushed against his arm, startling him.

"Hi, Rock," Tiffany purred.

With her inky shoulder-length tresses and her skin-tight white dress, which emphasized every curve and crevice, Tiffany would make most any man drown in drool. Unfortunately, she did nothing for Clint. Here was a stunning woman willing to give him full access to her considerable charms, but she left him dead cold. A woman who would probably run like a scalded cat if she knew he had a preteen daughter. Sonya had spoiled him for other women, in more ways than one. "Hi, Tiffany."

Batting her painted eyelids, she slid her arm through his and cooed, "I just love your house. It's so rustic and…cozy."

Pride swelled Clint's heart. "Thank you."

She traced a finger on his bare forearm. "Where do you live during the week?"

"Right here."

"Oooh." Tiffany winced and drew back. "You poor thing." She patted him on the arm. "I just couldn't survive this far from a shopping mall."

Before he could tell her no one had asked her to, he noticed Sonya and Neil standing at the foot of the wide steps. The expression on Sonya's face gave him some encouragement. She didn't look at all pleased to find Tiffany hanging over him. For one fleeting moment, he considered playing up to the model to make Sonya jealous, but discarded the idea. Unless Sonya came to him by her own choosing, he would respect her decision that they remain only friends.

Neil darted up the steps. "Tiff, Myles is talking about the upcoming movie he'll be directing." He crooked his arm. "I hear rumors of John Travolta. How about we join them?"

Straightening her dress, Tiffany blew Clint a kiss and took Neil's arm as she descended the steps, balancing on her skyscraper shoes. Sonya climbed the steps and stood beside him, her fresh-scrubbed scent wrapping around him as they watched the two maneuvre across the short-cropped grass.

In contrast to Tiffany's blatant sexuality, he found Sonya's subtle sensuality more potent. He craved the taste and feel of her skin. He envisioned using his lips and fingers to coax her passion free of its rigid shackles, to lead her to mindless pleasure with him. But he knew she wouldn't—couldn't—submit. And despite his frustration, he respected her reasons.

Neil turned and gave them a thumbs-up gesture.

Clint nodded in response. "That's what I call a timely rescue."

Sonya noted the deepening of the laugh crease beside Rock's mouth. A spurt of relief dissipated the jealousy she'd experienced at witnessing Tiffany's proximity to him. Like a moth lured by the very flame that could incinerate it, she was enticed by the irresistible power of the emotions and desire Rock evoked in her. Reckless, wild sensations.

Unable to resist the thrill of danger, she locked

gazes with him. "Neil thinks you and I should get together."

"Great minds think alike."

The desire in his eyes sucked her breath away; he wanted her. And not only her body yearned for him, her heart did, too. But love wasn't a luxury she could allow herself. Emotional dependence led to disaster. Her mother had sacrificed everything for unrequited passion—her career, her dignity and, finally, her life. Sonya wouldn't repeat her mother's mistake.

At least she had her career, and that's where she should focus her energies. The first phase of the campaign was almost completed and, given its initial success, she should discuss renewing Rock's contract. "I need to talk to you. Privately."

Rock cocked an eyebrow. "Anytime."

"How about after dinner?"

He reached out and tucked a lock of hair behind her ear. "It's a date."

His endearing gesture weakened her knees and threatened to weaken her resolve to concentrate on business. In an effort to avoid further temptation, Sonya stepped back. "Right now, I'm starving."

"How about a thick, juicy steak and a glass of red wine?"

She smiled gratefully. "Sounds like a fine idea."

"Okay, you get in line for the steak. I'll get you a glass of wine and meet you there."

A few minutes later, as Rock wove his way through the crowd toward her, Sonya noticed the easy manner with which he exchanged pleasantries with various members of her staff and the production crew.

His unexpected capability to integrate into her world intrigued her. What life experiences had shaped him? She admired his impressive physical attributes, but she also envied his steadfastness. Where she constantly strove for acceptance in her world, he was firmly rooted in his.

She craved to know more about this enigmatic cowboy whose life had touched her own in such an intimate way. Besides, the more she knew about him, the better her bargaining position would be.

"Thanks." She accepted the glass of wine from Rock and handed him a plate, half-filled with salads, before picking up her own. The enticing aroma of barbecued meat made her stomach rumble. "You're just in time to choose your steak. I wasn't sure how you liked it done."

He looked into her eyes. "Like most of the memorable things in life, it should be rare."

The rumble in her stomach grew louder. Only it wasn't her stomach. As Sonya glanced up, a helicopter whirred into view and descended into an empty corral.

"What the hell?"

Hearing the outrage in Rock's voice, Sonya bit her lip. Lawrence's and Harvey's unmistakable figures climbed out and headed toward them.

"Damn!" Rock snarled. "Couldn't they have chosen a less noticeable mode of transportation?"

Turning to him, Sonya lay a hand on his arm. "I'm sorry. I knew nothing about this. I'll speak to Lawrence about it."

Clint shook his head in resignation. "So much for a leisurely dinner."

Their chat would also have to be delayed. Chagrined, she set down her plate. "So much for dinner, period. Lawrence hates to be kept waiting."

Rock loped beside her as she hurried toward her boss. "Is our date still on for later?"

Her pulse quickened. "We'll have to play it by ear."

He flashed her a wicked grin. "I'll gladly play with your ear anytime."

A sinful thrill ran through her at the thought, followed closely by regret. If only the situation were different.

CLINT LED THEM into the high-beamed living room and gestured to the quartet of chunky, wood-framed armchairs at the far end of the room. They were clustered around a matching coffee table in front of the fieldstone fireplace. Harvey smiled in approval and waited for Sonya to slip into a chair before plunking his bulk down. Lawrence, with a fastidiousness that irritated Clint, brushed a hand over the coarse weave of the cushions as if he suspected creatures lurked there, before lowering himself into his chair's green depth.

Clint strode to his aged pine liquor cabinet. "Can I get you a drink?"

"Cognac, if you have it."

Clint ignored the condescending tone. "Would you prefer Courvoisier or Hennessey?"

Lawrence arched a brow. "How cosmopolitan of you. Courvoisier."

Refusing to be intimidated, Clint shook off the unease caused by Lawrence's penetrating gaze. The older man was up to something. They'd have to be on their toes. Plus the sooner they finished this discussion, the sooner he and Sonya could be alone.

Harvey grunted. "A shot of rye and seven would go down mighty fine."

Clint also poured Sonya a fresh glass of wine and himself another beer.

"Nice spread you've got here," Harvey boomed. "Prime real estate, in fact. Ever consider selling it?"

"No." Clint screwed the top back on the bottle of whiskey. "It's a legacy for my, uh, future generations."

"Let me know if you decide to sell." Harvey removed a cigar from his shirt pocket. "I'm in the market for a weekend retreat."

When Rock handed her the glass of wine, Sonya's gaze tangled with his. In her casual pants and sweater, she looked damned good sitting in his home, as if she belonged here. But the shoot was almost over, and she'd soon be leaving. His heart pinched at the realization he'd probably never see her again.

He distributed the remainder of the drinks, flicked on a floor lamp and table lamp and took the empty chair, which faced a large window. The sun's dying rays stained the scattered clouds, promising another day of unblemished weather.

"How is the shoot proceeding?" Lawrence asked, making a show of swirling the cognac.

"Excellent," Sonya enthused. "I'm very pleased with what we've shot so far. We should be wrapping up on schedule, the day after tomorrow."

"So, you're optimistic about the completed product?" Lawrence raised his snifter and, with a delicate sniff, inhaled the vapor.

Sonya leaned forward. "I'm confident we'll produce a commercial that will not only stand out, but will also deliver a significant market share."

Harvey removed a cigar from his shirt pocket. "Little lady, you're already a gol-darn genius. On the flight here, I was telling Lawrence that, so far, sales are quadruple what I had projected." He waggled the cigar in her direction. "There's a nice little bonus coming your way."

Sonya's eyes shone. "Thank you."

"Larry?" Harvey turned to his friend. "I want you to assign her to handle my national account, too."

Lawrence raised a palm. "Let's not be too hasty, Harv. We'll wait until the whole project's completed before determining whether she's ready for the increased responsibility."

An aura of menace prowled behind the facade of MacLeod's benign smile. Clint's skin crawled. He'd bet his ranch Sonya was the chosen prey.

She smiled at Harvey. "I can't take all the credit for the campaign's success. Without Rock, none of this would have been possible."

"That's true." Harvey turned his attention to Clint. "Son, I want to renew your contract for two years, at five times the rate you're being paid now. 'Course, I expect exclusivity of your services in the clothing market."

The generosity of the offer stunned Clint. As much as he would have welcomed the money, he couldn't risk the long-term exposure. Sooner or later something or someone would give him away, then Tia would suffer the consequences. He hoped his refusal wouldn't have a negative impact on Sonya's career. "Thank you, sir, that's very generous. But I can't possibly accept it."

"Why on earth not?" Harvey blustered, throwing a puzzled glance at Lawrence, then Sonya.

"Harvey, you've given Rock quite a surprise." Sonya's smile didn't quite reach her eyes. "I'd appreciate having some time to discuss your proposal with him in private."

Was she in on this, too? Was it a Zenith Communications negotiation tactic to throw him off balance? Clint wasn't going to be railroaded into agreeing to anything. "Look, I only agreed to a one-shot deal. I can't commit myself to two years."

"Zenith Communications generously gave you an opportunity and met your terms." Lawrence's smile was ice-cold. "I think the least you can do is consider the negative impact such action would have on Rocky Ridge blue jeans."

Harvey harrumphed. "You mean he can walk away from this deal?"

"The standard renewal clause was deleted from the contract." Lawrence waved a hand at Clint. "So, basically, we're at Rock's mercy." He shifted his gaze to Sonya. "Poor planning, my dear."

Sonya stared, her chin in the air. "Given the circumstances at the time, it was the best, and only, decision I could make."

Cold anger burned in Clint's veins. MacLeod was carefully mounting an ambush against Sonya. "Don't blame Sonya. I insisted on the removal of the clause."

Lawrence gave a casual shrug. "Then why don't we simply find another Rocky Ridge man?"

Sonya's wineglass slapped against the wooden surface of an end table. "Impossible. We've established a powerful presence with Rock. It would be difficult, if not impossible, to duplicate his body language. And even though most of his face is shadowed, people would still be able to tell it wasn't the same man. If we replace him, we could jeopardize the entire success of the campaign."

"And I'm not interested in changing horses in mid-stream." Harvey turned to Clint. "Son, you can't back out on us now. I've never seen anything like it. People are goin' crazy tryin' to guess who the Rocky Ridge man is. The gals in my office are flooded with calls from radio stations, newspapers, television talk shows and magazines, all offering me big money if I reveal your identity."

"I had no idea the response had grown to that proportion," Sonya murmured.

Clint's heart quickened. "What have you told them?"

"As little as possible." Harvey rubbed his hands together. "The mystery is drivin' them insane, but it's great for business."

"The intense media interest also means we have to proceed carefully." Lawrence propped his fingers beneath his chin. "This whole thing has grown too big, too fast."

"As the account executive in charge of this project, I'd like some time to review the situation, project the impact of various scenarios and make my recommendations to you," Sonya interjected in a firm voice.

"It's dangerous if we don't take immediate action." Lawrence stroked his mustache and turned to Sonya. "I know I've given you free rein, my dear. But as president of Zenith Communications, it's my responsibility to ensure our client receives our most senior expertise in this matter. Therefore, I'll assume leadership of this project. And before this whole situation backfires on Rocky Ridge blue jeans, I recommend we reveal Rock's identity."

Clint's mind reeled under the impact of MacLeod's words, as fear arrowed to his heart. Shooting Sonya a quick look, he noted the shock on her face as she gaped at her boss. Finally, he punched a single word past the panic that strangled his throat. "No!"

"We can't." Sonya spoke firmly. "The contract prohibits us from doing so, unless we have Rock's permission."

The constriction in Clint's throat eased. "And I refuse to give my permission."

"There'll be big money in it for you, Rock. The publicity will be tremendous. Harvey will send you on a promotional tour to each Rocky Ridge store. Make you a household name."

Clint fumed. MacLeod's arrogance infuriated him. Couldn't Sonya see what her boss was doing? Now that the campaign was proving a success, MacLeod had taken control of it by using her desire for the vice presidency to ensure her compliance. There was only one tactic at Clint's disposal. He had to stall for time, talk to Sonya and convince her to stand up against MacLeod. "Listen, Sonya is the only person I'm going to discuss this—"

A muffled sneeze drew his attention to the arched entrance to the room. Tia stood there, a guilty expression on her face. "Hi, Dad." Her eyes scanned the room. "Hi, Sonya."

Everything was falling apart. "Hi, sweetheart. What are you doing here?"

Her eyes sparkled with excitement. "Katie and I were out ridin'—" she beckoned her friend, "—and we saw the helicopter land, so we came over to see what was happenin'."

Before Clint could form a reply, Harvey addressed the girls. "Would you little ladies like to take a ride in it tomorrow morning?"

"Could we?" Two innocent faces, bright with natural curiosity and eagerness, focused on him. "Please, Daddy, please?"

Clint considered his options. Night had descended, so he couldn't send the girls back to Katie's house tonight by horseback. If he drove them over now, it meant denying them the excitement of the helicopter ride, and he'd still have to make arrangements for them to return for the horses tomorrow. Bad idea. He was scheduled in front of the camera all day. Besides, he needed to talk to Sonya immediately, and the girls' presence was the perfect excuse for terminating this discussion. "All right." He stood. "Let's go call Katie's parents and get you settled for the night. But you'll have to ride back to Katie's house right after the helicopter ride tomorrow."

"Sure, Dad."

"Okay, Mr. Silver."

"Excuse me, gentlemen." He addressed Sonya. "We'll meet in private later?"

Sonya's eyes appeared bruised with fatigue, but she nodded. "Of course."

Dread gnawed at Clint. Sonya was his only potential ally. He had to ask her to defy her boss and possibly jeopardize her promotion and her very career to help him. If she didn't, the media would gorge on the unveiling of the Rocky Ridge man, with the scandal of the past serving as a succulent dessert. Tia's world would shatter. He had to prevent that from happening.

Yet, against all reason, he'd developed impossible feelings for Sonya and was sure she cared for him. He'd seen it in her eyes, felt it in the response of her body. God help him if he was forced to choose between his daughter's happiness...or Sonya's.

As ROCK USHERED the two girls out of the room, Lawrence refreshed his and Harvey's drinks. Meanwhile, Sonya struggled to comprehend what had just taken place. For the past week she'd been isolated on the ranch, engrossed in the task at hand. In bed after midnight, and up before dawn, she'd touched base with Lawrence daily, but he hadn't conveyed any news about increased media interest in the Rocky Ridge project. Had he deliberately kept her in the dark or was this another test of her abilities?

Guilt's heavy hand squeezed her conscience. She'd allowed herself to be distracted by her feelings for Rock, proof she was her mother's daughter. As a result, she'd lost ground, and now, she'd have to prove she could manage the situation. Like a vice president of Zenith Communications would.

Regardless of anyone else's actions, the ultimate responsibility for the campaign was hers. Sonya swallowed and directed her attention to her boss. "I apologize. I should've been on top of the media situation."

Lawrence snapped his electronic notebook shut. "I expect my senior personnel to have the foresight to anticipate such scenarios and prepare appropriate strategies."

She raised her chin. "It would have helped if I'd been kept informed of the situation."

Lawrence's upper lip curled. "It's always a mistake to rely too heavily on others."

Even her own boss. "I see that now."

"Now, don't you worry, little lady." Harvey's kind

eyes were reassuring. "You've had your hands full, and you've done a superb job. 'Sides, Larry here has to earn his extravagant salary, too."

Her smile wobbled. "I appreciate your confidence, Harvey. In order to control the media hype and preserve the original concept of the campaign, there is one other option we could consider."

"What's that, little lady?"

"Rather than reveal Rock's identity, we could ease off on the campaign a bit, let things cool down and delay the introduction of the television commercials. Then, when the timing is right, we can rekindle the consumer's curiosity."

"There's a severe downside to that strategy. Sales could drop off too much." Lawrence drained his cognac. "I recommend striking while the iron is hot."

Harvey thumped a meaty hand on the arm of his chair. "If you can persuade Rock to agree, I'll add another iron to the fire. With all the hoopla, I'm gonna move up my plans to expand the Rocky Ridge line to include children's jeans. How's about using his daughter as a model? They could make appearances together."

Visually, the pair would be stunning. "It's a fantastic idea." Sonya shook her head. "But Rock won't go for it."

Harvey leaned back, linking his fingers over his paunch. "Why not?"

"I've already mentioned the possibility of using Tia as a model, but he informed me it wasn't something he'd consider."

"Then I'll offer him more money."

Sonya chose her words with care. "I don't think it's a question of money."

"Then what?"

Sonya sighed. "He doesn't want his daughter subjected to that kind of life-style."

"Convince him." Lawrence's voice dripped with condescension. "Zenith Communications expects its executives to put our clients' interests first. If you can't bring a simple cowboy in line, I will seriously question your ability to contribute any further to this company. I want an answer tomorrow."

Fear froze Sonya's heart. Lawrence wouldn't accept defeat, and Rock had been equally adamant about not revealing his identity. As an employee of Zenith Communications, she owed the company her loyalty; yet, as a representative of Zenith, she'd made a promise to Rock. But if she didn't persuade him to reveal himself as the Rocky Ridge man, she'd not only lose her promotion, she'd lose her job.

Her job represented stability, survival. It demonstrated her success in rising above the circumstances that had claimed her mother.

Appealing to Lawrence was useless; he would be merciless. Rock was her only hope. There had to be a way to persuade him to reveal his identity.

12

CLINT INHALED a deep breath of the night air, heavy with the perfumed scent of clover. The velvet glove of night closed around them as he and Sonya leaned over the veranda rail. After spending a hectic hour supervising the girls and preparing the guest rooms, he'd discovered Sonya had retreated to the kitchen to reheat their steak dinners. They'd discussed the day's shoot over their meal, then retired to the veranda.

Due to their early call the next morning, the majority of the crew had withdrawn to their quarters. Only the odd muffled laugh and a hint of music drifted across the dark ranch yard.

"It's incredible how many stars there are here," Sonya murmured.

Weariness weighed heavily on him. Why did life have to be so complex? Why couldn't they be sweethearts, sharing the romance of a beautiful summer night? "That's because there're no office towers blocking the view here. We ranchers prefer starlight to streetlights."

"It's a totally different world out here."

Clint listened to the sharp screech of a nighthawk, finding reassurance in the knowledge that regardless of the unpredictability of humans, nature carried on. "To me, this is real."

"Isn't reality whatever you make it?" He heard the smile in her voice.

"Then I guess we've created a monster." He shook his head. "This whole Rocky Ridge man persona has gotten out of hand."

"A major media monster." Sonya's hand touched his. "I'm sorry."

His hand tingled from the contact. "For what?"

"That I didn't keep better control of it."

Exasperation bit into Clint. "How could you? You can't be expected to do everything yourself. You've been working sixteen-hour days!"

She shrugged. "That's the name of the advertising game."

"I think MacLeod's dangling the vice presidency in front of you like a carrot, and because you're determined to prove yourself, you keep jumping through hoops for him. Haven't you noticed he keeps changing the rules of the game?"

Sonya swiveled to face him. "He's testing me, that's all. If I give in, I lose the vice presidency. Whether he takes the credit or not, bottom line, the project is my responsibility."

"I shouldn't have pushed the idea on you."

"No, you were absolutely right. The idea is brilliant."

He ached to caress her earnest face. "The world's full of ideas. You made it work."

Bitterness laced Sonya's laugh as she turned away. "I never knew there could be such a thing as being too successful."

"Believe me, too much success can be just as devastating as failure, maybe even worse."

"You sound as though you're speaking from experience."

Clint tilted his head and stared into the inky blackness beyond the stars. "Witnessing success born from failure can be inspiring, but witnessing failure due to the death of success is heartbreaking. You have to decide what price you're willing to pay."

She crossed her arms. "I've worked too hard to fail now."

Clint swung to face her. "You agree with them, about revealing my identity. Don't you?"

She licked her lips before replying. "It doesn't matter what I think anymore. Lawrence has decided he's calling the shots."

"But I want to know what *you* think."

She tossed her head. "All right. It's my professional opinion that the publicity we've created has taken on a life of its own. We're not at the controls anymore. I see two options. If the situation isn't at a critical point, we can ease back on the advertising until the excitement dies down a little, then feed the mystery a little more. If the strategy and its reactions are carefully monitored, the momentum can be controlled."

He grasped at the hope revealed by her words. "Will MacLeod go for it?"

"I tried. He refused."

"And the second option?"

"The only way to regain immediate control is to seize it, by doing what Lawrence suggested—revealing your identity."

The resignation in her voice triggered Clint's alarm. "You know I can't take the risk."

"No." Her eyes dropped to her hands. "I only know you *say* you can't."

"You don't believe me."

Her head snapped up. "How the hell can you expect me to? My job is all I have, and if I'm fired from such a high profile project, I'll never be able to find a job in this industry again. Lawrence will make sure of that."

The obvious emotion in her voice staggered him. In response, he stepped closer to her. "If I could reveal my identity, I would. You have to believe me."

In the dim light her eyes were huge pools of desperation. "It's not a question of belief—it's gone way beyond that. We're down to necessity. I need my job, you need the money."

Clint held her gaze. "I only agreed to this job so I could save my ranch and preserve a stable life-style for my daughter."

"Tia made quite an impression on Harvey. I've also been asked to arrange for her to model the new line of Rocky Ridge childrens' jeans."

"What the hell have I gotten myself into?" Fear ignited his fury. "They're insatiable. Well, they don't own me, and I'll never allow them to touch my daughter!" With the heel of his hand, he thumped the veranda rail in frustration. There was only one way out of the situation. "Tell them if they pursue this matter, they'll lose more than they'll gain."

His outburst forced Sonya to step back. "What do you mean?"

"If my identity is revealed, you'll have an even greater media disaster on your hands."

SONYA'S NERVES and patience stretched fiber thin. "For God's sake, Rock! Tell me why!"

He whipped around, his grim face looming over her. "Because of who I am."

His intensity frightened her. "Who are you?" she whispered.

"Do you remember Winter Olympics that were held in Calgary?"

"Vaguely." She steadied herself against a veranda post. "I was in university at the time, and working part-time. Why?"

"I competed in the games as a downhill skier." His words were clipped. "Does the name Quicksilver ring a bell?"

She frowned in concentration, then realization dawned. "You're the guy everyone was talking about. The whiz kid from the States, whose parents were killed on the way to the last competition before the Olympics. You vowed to win for them, and you were the favorite for the gold medal, but you crashed on the final run."

Turning toward her, he raised his hands in a gesture of surrender. "That's me. Clint Silver." His eyes bored into hers. "And my late wife was Kristin King."

"Oh, my God. The supermodel." Sonya recalled the fiery hair, pouty face and impossibly thin body that had graced the covers of fashion magazines. "She created a stir by posing almost nude when she was pregnant."

Rock thrust his hands into his jeans pockets. "Kristin craved the limelight. Couldn't get enough of it." He turned and stared into the darkness. "Couldn't live without it."

Sonya remembered the newspaper headlines about the supermodel who, after her pregnancy, had posed again, this time completely nude for a men's magazine. The media had had a field day. Soon after, Kristin had been arrested for possession of cocaine. "Wasn't she one of the jet set who overdosed on the yacht in the Mediterranean?"

Rock's shoulders hunched. "Her, a couple of rock stars and a Lord something-or-other. They offered her a more glamorous life-style than a has-been skier and an infant daughter. Kristin wanted to live an illusion."

Sonya's heart contracted in sympathy. She moved to his side, her instinct to offer physical comfort inhibited by Rock's constraint. She laced her fingers together and spoke from her heart. "I'm so sorry. Your loss must have been overwhelming."

"I'd lost her long before that. Kristin couldn't deal with illness or physical imperfection. I'd been sure that, once my ski injuries healed, things would be better again. I was wrong." He straightened his shoulders. "Tia was the best thing that came out of our marriage. Her birth was the result of one of our attempts at reconciliation. It didn't work. Kristin left us when Tia was four months old."

Sonya's eyes filled. "Poor Tia."

Rock turned, his face a mask of pain. "She doesn't know about her mother. I thought it would be best to wait until she was older. She'll be devastated." His gaze devoured Sonya's. "I won't allow Tia's life to be tainted by what Kristin did."

Sonya nodded. "That's why you're against Tia modeling."

Rock sighed and rubbed a hand across his face. "She's so much like her mother."

"Maybe in her looks, but I see a lot of you in her. I

can understand why you're protective of her, but she may be able to handle things better than you think."

"She's not ready." Rock folded his arms across his chest. "If my identity is revealed, the media will resurrect the whole mess. I won't put Tia through that hell."

The futility of her situation made Sonya feel numb with lost hope. "And now I'm left with a hell of a decision to make. I knew from the start you would be trouble, cowboy." She turned her back on him, shaking her head dully. "I just didn't know how much."

"I'm sorry I didn't tell you all this up front, but if I had, you'd never have hired me. Rocky Ridge blue jeans wouldn't have wanted my sordid story associated with their product. And I'd have lost the ranch." He laid a hand on her shoulder. "It was a rotten choice, but the only one I could make."

Her emotions in turmoil, Sonya shrugged his hand off. "In this situation, all the choices are rotten."

"What are you going to do?"

She turned to face him, struggling for the right answer within herself even as she jutted her chin and said, "My best."

Rock stepped closer, his intensity a palpable force. "I'd never ask you to jeopardize your job on my behalf but, for Tia's sake, I'm begging you not to tell Lawrence who I am."

Her world fell apart. "That information may be the only way for me to save my job."

The torment in his eyes imprisoned her. "The choice is yours to make."

THE NEXT DAY, as the sun succumbed to the evening's embrace, Sonya mounted the steps to the ranch house. With each slap of her sandals against the floor-boards of the veranda, trepidation knotted her stomach. As much as she wanted to, she couldn't delay responding to Lawrence's terse summons, delivered via cellular phone.

She'd come directly from the location, where they were finally wrapping up for the night. It'd been a tough day. In addition to Rock's lack of concentration, which had resulted in a larger than expected number of takes, her own mind had kept wandering to his revelations of last night.

Opening the front door of the ranch house, she took a deep breath. The situation was impossible. If she didn't reveal Rock's identity, she'd lose her job and reputation—everything she'd ever worked for. She'd lose her battle to prove she could overcome the legacy of her past.

And if she revealed Rock's identity, she'd risk causing irreparable emotional damage to an innocent child and her father. The man whom, against her better judgment, she'd come to love. History would repeat itself; just as Kristin had, Sonya would sacrifice everything in pursuit of her own desires. All night she'd tossed and turned, trying to find a mutually satisfactory compromise, without success.

She walked down the hallway to Rock's study, where Lawrence had told her he'd wait. The only thing she could do at this point would be to stall Lawrence until the shoot was completed tomorrow. That way, at least Rock would receive his money, and she would buy more time to find a solution to the publicity problem. Hopefully Neil, who was researching the subject from the privacy of their motor home, would uncover support for the option she'd already proposed or would turn up a new alternative.

Lawrence sat at a scarred desk, his laptop computer open, while the well-groomed cast of a popular situation comedy cavorted on the muted television nearby. A small smile skulked around Lawrence's lips as he spoke into his cellular phone. "We'll address that at our press conference in the morning. Until then, you have our statement." He snapped the phone closed and gestured to a chair next to him. "Sit down."

Sonya obeyed, hoping he'd invited her here for a reason other than discussing the Rocky Ridge campaign.

"Have you secured Rock's agreement on revealing his identity to the media?"

She drew a deep breath. "Is it possible I can have a little more time?"

Lawrence sneered. "He wouldn't agree to it."

"Not yet."

"Why not?"

She clasped her hands in a knot. "He has important personal reasons that prevent him from giving me the permission we need."

"Such as?"

"I can't say. But I have reason to feel that it would not be in the best interest of Rocky Ridge to reveal the truth."

"Why?"

"Again, I can't say."

His eyes, cold as blue steel, scrutinized her. "Can't, or won't?"

Pressing her lips together, she stared back at him.

Lawrence relaxed in his chair, an odd smile on his

thin lips. "I'm disappointed in you, Sonya. You've allowed emotion to supersede your business judgment. I thought I'd trained you better than that."

"You had. But when you assigned me independent status on the Rocky Ridge project, I guess I took you literally."

"I had great faith in you, Sonya. I'd hoped you would set an example of conduct for other aspiring female executives. However, I don't believe you are acting in the best interest of either Zenith Communications or our client, Rocky Ridge blue jeans."

Instead of gouging her self-confidence, the words rolled harmlessly off her new mantle of composure. "I disagree, Lawrence. I think Zenith Communications' professional image has been significantly enhanced by the creative campaign we've launched on behalf of Rocky Ridge."

Lawrence tsked. "And I thought you'd learned your lesson with the Saunders' proposal."

"Recently, I've done a lot of thinking about their defection to our competitors. I don't believe they ever saw my proposal. I think you replaced it with a more conservative concept, which they rejected. Didn't you?"

Lawrence dismissed her declaration with a wave of his hand. "Of course I did. I couldn't risk our reputation on an unproven concept."

All these years, she'd been preserving a one-sided loyalty. Zenith had initially appealed to her because of its stability and security when, in fact, it was stagnating in its antiquated corporate culture. Zenith hadn't kept pace with change. And neither had Lawrence. The man she'd considered her mentor had inhibited her growth. And, because of her own fear, she'd allowed herself to be convinced of his infallibility.

Meanwhile, Rock had prompted her to take risks, to seek her own truth. The future lay in innovation, not in imitation of the past. The knowledge released her burden, and an incredible sense of freedom spilled through her. She owed nothing to Lawrence, or Zenith. Or to the memory of her mother. Only to herself. And Rock. All she had to do was prove it.

She stood, forcing Lawrence to look up at her. "We have a contract with Rock, and I'll resign before I break it."

He snorted. "Typical female weakness. Nothing more than I should have expected."

"You're wrong, Lawrence." A flash of certainty generated her smile of triumph. "It's not a typical female weakness. It's a special female strength."

"Whatever." He examined his Rolex watch. "That's why I took matters into my own hands."

Dread chilled her soul. "What are you talking about?"

"Take a look." His thumb punched a button on the remote control device.

The intro to a news program faded and the popular female anchor smiled. A close-up of a much younger Rock materialized, then was replaced by a present-day photo as a female reporter identified him as Clint Silver. Revealing him as the Rocky Ridge man, she detailed his professional and personal history. "Oh, my God."

"Such carelessness, Sonya, to allow an unauthorized photo to be circulated."

"But, I didn't. We counted each roll of..." A photo of Kristin King, an older version of Tia, filled the screen. Appalled, Sonya whispered, "Do you have any idea what you've done?"

"Me?" Lawrence chuckled. "Oh, no. Unbeknown to us, a renegade young account executive named Sonya Duncan undertook this action by her own initiative. Of course, Zenith Communications did not authorize this action and is most disappointed she took matters into her own hands." He shook his head in mock sympathy. "No doubt she cracked under the stress of trying to handle such a high-profile campaign. We're holding a news conference in the morning to inform the public we've taken appropriate action by releasing Ms. Duncan from her duties with Zenith Communications."

Dumbfounded, Sonya stared at Lawrence. "Why?"

"Survival." He emitted a loud sigh. "You were getting too close, my dear. The next thing you know, you'd be setting your sights on the presidency of Zenith Communications. I couldn't allow that."

Her mind whirling, Sonya tried to focus on tangibles. "How did you discover Rock's identity?"

"*I* did my homework. Last night, Tia's little friend called him Mr. Silver. This morning, during the helicopter ride, I asked Tia what her dad's first name was. The name Clint Silver rang a bell, so I put my assistant on it. Of course, the tie-in to Kristin King was irresistible."

"You used *children* for your own gain?" Her anger propelled her to her feet. "You're a despicable coward, Lawrence." She leaned over the desk and stared him straight in the eyes. "I'm not going to let you destroy the two people I love."

"My, my. Such passion, my dear. How uncivilized.

It's a dangerous commodity that has no place in business."

"That's where I'm going to prove you wrong, Lawrence." As she left him, the smirk was fading from his face.

Sonya had to find Rock, explain Lawrence's treachery. Together, they'd figure out what to do. As she reached the end of the hallway, she almost barreled into him. "Thank God! I need to talk to you."

The ice-cold contempt in his eyes impaled her heart. "I think the newscast said it all." A harsh laugh contorted his features. "My mistake was in thinking you were different from the others."

"Please, let me explain—"

His face hardened. "You made your choice."

"Please, Rock, I lo—"

"You know, I'm a big enough fool that I might have been able to forgive your betrayal of me, but I'll never forgive you for betraying Tia."

A part of her, new and vibrant, died. "Where are you going?"

"I'm taking Tia away until everything quiets down. When I get back, I want all traces of you and your associates gone." He hefted a rucksack over his shoulder. "I trust you can arrange that, Ms. Duncan."

Rock strode to the front door and walked out of her life.

13

SONYA HUDDLED on the veranda steps, her arms wrapped around her knees, which were tucked up against her chest. Feeling as empty and lifeless as a dried corn husk, she stared sightlessly at the stars. Rock, the man she loved, had just accused her of betraying him and his daughter.

She didn't blame him for holding her responsible; regardless of who had actually released the information, the promise she'd made to him was broken. So was the tender sprig of hope she'd dared to begin nourishing, the possibility that they could have a future together. The look in Rock's eyes when he'd said he'd never forgive her still haunted her.

Small wonder he'd ordered her and her associates to leave. Muted sounds of laughter and music drifted from the direction of the motor homes. With Rock gone, they'd have to abandon the shoot. Without finishing the campaign, he wouldn't get paid. Rock would lose his ranch.

No! She couldn't allow that to happen. There had to be a way to salvage this whole mess, to keep Rock and Tia from losing their home. She wouldn't ruin the lives of the two people she loved. But what could she do? Appealing to Lawrence to pay out Rock's unfulfilled contract would be useless; her former boss was legendary for his ruthlessness. She could offer Rock her own savings, yet she knew he would never accept. There was only one option. She had to talk to Harvey. It was a long shot, but it was her only shot.

Minutes later, Sonya found Harvey and Lawrence in the living room, deep in conversation. They both looked up as she approached. While worry engraved every fold of Harvey's face, Lawrence cast her a disdainful smile. She had to convince Harvey to listen to her, before her former boss totally poisoned his mind. "Excuse me, Harvey, could I speak to you in private?"

Before Harvey could reply, Lawrence held up a hand. "We're in the middle of a crisis situation here. I've just informed Harvey about Rock's sordid identity, so it's most urgent that we immediately discuss its impact on Rocky Ridge blue jeans."

"Looks like we'll need all the help we can get." Harvey's voice was minus its usual vitality. "Have a seat, little lady."

Obviously Lawrence hadn't informed him she'd been fired. Sonya hesitated. What she had to say was for Harvey's ears only.

Lawrence seized advantage of her inaction. "Yes, I'd be *most* interested in what Sonya has to say."

So that was his strategy. By being privy to the discussion, Lawrence would attempt to control the situation and eliminate any opportunity for her to influence Harvey. It wouldn't be easy to outline her proposal with Lawrence ready to refute everything. She'd just have to beat him at his own game. Sonya sat next to Harvey, across from Lawrence. "I'd be happy to share my ideas with you. But, in deference to Lawrence's position as president of Zenith Communications, I must insist he take the lead, and give us the benefit of his expertise."

When Lawrence's eyes narrowed in response, a spark of triumph ignited inside Sonya. He knew his refusal would imply that her opinion took precedence over his.

Lawrence sat back and crossed his ankles. "Drawing on my years of experience, I recommend that we minimize damage by dissociating ourselves from Clint Silver, aka Rock. We'll issue an immediate statement that we had no knowledge of Rock's true identity, and denounce him as the Rocky Ridge man. To avoid any further scandal, we will pull all current advertisements and halt production on those already in the works. After the furor has died down, we'll redesign a completely new campaign, with a more suitable candidate as the Rocky Ridge man."

"In other words, we claim he hoodwinked us." Harvey rubbed the side of his nose for a moment, then turned to Sonya. "What do you think, little lady?"

"In the *past,* that would have been the preferred solution." Sonya leaned toward Harvey, intent in her conviction. "But today, the public wants corporations to be more humane. I suggest Rocky Ridge blue jeans embrace this opportunity and endorse Clint as someone who has made great strides in overcoming adversity. We can highlight his Olympic struggle, plus the challenges he faces in running a ranch while raising a daughter on his own. We show him as the hero he is."

Harvey nodded. "I think you've got something there."

Lawrence thrust himself forward in his chair. "We can't trust her, Harv. As the executive in charge, she bungled this project—first by hiring Rock, then by failing to keep his identity secret. Besides, I've already fired her."

Harvey turned to Sonya. "Is this true?"

"Yes. And I'm willing to accept responsibility for whatever happened while I was directing the campaign."

Lawrence smiled in satisfaction. "I should hope so."

At that moment, she knew she had him. "However, I'm compelled to point out that I was no longer in charge of the project when Rock's identity was revealed." Sonya gestured toward her former boss. "Yesterday, Lawrence relieved me of that duty... when he assumed leadership of the project."

"Now, wait just a minute—"

"She's right, Larry. That was just before Rock's daughter interrupted our meeting."

Color tinged Lawrence's prominent cheekbones. He waved a hand in dismissal. "Whatever. What's important is that we apply all of Zenith's extensive resources to addressing this situation. Sonya, you're excused."

Harvey lumbered to his feet. "No, Larry, I'm afraid you're the one who's leaving. From where I stand, Sonya was the one responsible for the success of my campaign." Harvey shook his head, a look of disgust on his face. "You don't even have the balls to back up your own people, or admit it when you're wrong."

Hope revived in Sonya's heart.

Lawrence stood, his outrage evident. "May I remind you there is a contractual agreement between Rocky Ridge blue jeans and Zenith Communications?"

"No. 'Cause if you do, I'll sue your ass for breach of contract."

Indignation vibrated from Lawrence's rigid posture. "No big loss," he sneered.

Sonya smiled. "You know what they say, Lawrence. Bad news travels fast."

Harvey waited until Lawrence left the room, before turning to Sonya. He winked. "I've got a proposition for you, little lady."

DAYLIGHT PEARLED the granite peaks that thrust toward the heavens. Clint turned from the window of the one-room cabin and fed the greedy fire in the woodstove, then filled a kettle with water and set it to boil. In the dim light, his gaze caressed the slight form curled up in her sleeping bag.

Tia had been bursting with a thousand questions last night when he'd gone to get her at Katie's ranch, but it'd been late when they'd arrived at the cabin, and he'd put off answering her until morning. She would soon wake up and, although he'd spent the entire night without sleep, thinking of all that had happened, of all that needed to be said, the one image that remained in his mind was the ravaged expression on Sonya's face.

The television report had claimed the information had been leaked by Sonya, and in his shock, he'd reacted without thinking, his attention focused on protecting Tia. But sometime during the dark, forlorn hours of the night he'd begun to question the accuracy of the report.

Sonya had demonstrated her integrity time and time again; she'd even put her concern for Tia ahead of her own physical desires. His inability to trust her didn't stem from her character or actions. It was because of his guilt over Kristin, his shame in being unable to protect his wife from her destructive addictions.

His guilt had prevented him from seeing what was now so clear—he loved Sonya. After he talked to Tia, he'd find Sonya and apologize for his behavior, explain that it hadn't been her he'd distrusted, but himself. He'd find a way to make things right. He loved her too much to let her go. Maybe in time, she'd forgive him and come to love him too.

"Mornin', Dad."

"Hi, sweetheart."

Tia yawned and sat up, her copper locks rippling. Her wide blue eyes inspected his face. "You don't look angry anymore. You look sad."

She looked so much like her mother, yet she was so unlike her in personality. Where Kristin had been self-absorbed, Tia was considerate of others. Maybe Sonya was right—his fear had blinded him to his daughter's sensibility and had caused him to restrict her growth. He smiled into Tia's clear eyes. "I have to talk to you about your mother."

THE UP-TEMPO BEAT of the country rock tune on the convertible's stereo thrummed through Sonya. Despite her healthy disregard for the speed limit, the kilometers dragged by as she inched toward the mountain peaks. Over the weekend, she'd returned to Calgary and worked hard on the new campaign for Rocky Ridge blue jeans, employing every single available resource. Neil had been invaluable, cashing in on all the favors owed to them both.

The cheque in her briefcase, made out to Rock,

should be sufficient not only to save his ranch, but also to ensure some degree of financial stability for him and Tia. The money could never make up for the anguish they'd suffered, but she'd never have been able to live with the knowledge that she'd been responsible for the loss of their ranch. She'd also enclosed a personal note expressing her regret at what had happened.

She didn't know when Rock and Tia would return home. But when they did the cheque would be waiting under their door, along with an offer that also signaled an exciting new direction for her career.

An exhilarating sense of freedom washed through her. This way they'd all be able to start anew, and maybe, in time, Rock would forgive her, maybe even learn to trust her. Her heart clenched. Love couldn't exist without trust—Rock had taught her that. Until then, she'd wait, as her mother had waited before her. But she wouldn't drown in despair—that was the difference between her and her mother. Sonya had let go of the debilitating past in her professional life and she was determined to do the same in her personal life.

As she turned into the entrance of the Silver S Ranch, a bright red-and-white sign caught her eye. For Sale. Rock was selling his ranch. Because of her, he and Tia were being driven from their home. She pressed the accelerator, ignoring the jouncing motion of the car.

"Where are you, Sonya?" Rock's familiar rasp emanated from the radio. Stunned, Sonya swerved to a stop and stared at the dashboard of her car. Her heart bounced off the walls of her chest. What was he doing?

"Some of you may remember that, a few weeks

ago, I interviewed a beautiful lady on the air—an advertising executive searching for Rock, the man she wanted to represent Rocky Ridge blue jeans." The rich baritone voice chuckled. "Today, we're talking by phone to Clint Silver, the infamous Rocky Ridge man, who's on a search of his own.

"Mr. Silver, let's start at the beginning. Earlier this week, after the news of your identity broke, you dropped out of sight. Why?"

"My daughter was unaware of the circumstances surrounding the death of her mother, Kristin King. I wanted some privacy to tell her myself."

"And why are you here today?"

"After we discussed the matter, Tia asked me if we could try to prevent the same thing from happening to other young people, by telling them what had happened to her mother."

"You must be proud of your daughter."

"I am very proud and I—" Rock's voice cracked. He cleared his throat. "I'm humbled by her generosity."

Emotion clogged Sonya's throat. If Tia could accept her mother's faults, why couldn't she do the same?

"Mr. Silver, why is it so important you find Ms. Duncan?"

"Tia and I need her."

Sonya's heartbeat stalled.

"Oh? What exactly do you need her for?"

"Ms. Duncan managed the Rocky Ridge project, and I'd like her to undertake a new project for us."

"Thank you. We've been speaking to Clint Silver—"

Sonya turned the radio off, put the car in gear and continued down the drive. Hope bloomed in her heart. He'd said they wanted her. Was he ready to forgive her? Granted, it was only her professional services Rock was interested in, but that was a start.

She pulled up in front of the ranch house and pushed the trunk-release button. Stepping out into the morning sun, she wiped her sweaty palms on her khaki shorts. Songbirds praised the summer-scented morning, while bees browsed the tangled clumps of pink, fragrant wild roses that fringed the base of the veranda. The house was silent, the front door closed. They weren't home.

The trepidation she'd nursed faded and was chased by disappointment. Although she risked encountering Rock's wrath for what he believed had been her betrayal, she yearned simply to be near him. Without his lopsided grin and his stolid presence, vitality had disappeared from her life.

As she reached into the trunk for her briefcase, her hand brushed against the snowy white Stetson Rock had given her. She picked it up and ran a palm over its firm crown. In the past, cowboy hats had symbolized loss and despair, but through Rock she'd gained a new perspective. Today, its sturdy structure embodied hope and friendship, and a distant promise of trust and love.

Startled by the sound of a door slamming, she spun around, the Stetson dangling from one hand. The cowboy of her dreams had materialized on the veranda. Her love swelled at the sight of his denim-clad physique, his rugged face. How could she maintain a professional relationship with this man, when what she longed for was the magic of his arms? Her mouth dry, her heart pounding, she watched him descend the steps toward her, exuding taut masculinity with every movement.

When Clint saw Sonya in his yard, he almost dropped his coffee. Astonishment, joy and fear collided in his heart. He craved to fold her in his arms, to never let her go, but the uncertain expression on her face and the Stetson in her hand held him back.

Had she come here to return his gift? He wouldn't blame her after the way he'd treated her. He set his mug down on the veranda rail. Hopefully, she'd give him a chance to make it up to her. He had to handle this properly. If he could reestablish a business relationship, court her slowly, show her that he and Tia could fit into her world, perhaps friendship would follow. Then maybe, one day, she'd come to love him as much as he loved her. He stood, an arm's length in front of her. "Sonya."

She raised the Stetson and clasped it against her midriff. "Rock." Anguish stung him at the note of caution in her voice.

"I—" They spoke simultaneously.

Clint halved the distance between them. "Please, let me go first."

She nodded, her fingers kneading the brim of the hat.

"I'm sorry I blamed you for revealing my identity." He held her gaze, determined to erase the tangle of emotions visible in her eyes. "After I had time to think about it, I knew it had to be MacLeod's doing, not yours. When we got back to the ranch, I tried to call you to apologize, but you'd moved out of your hotel, and Zenith's phone number has been disconnected."

"I resigned, even before I knew what Lawrence had done. And Harvey fired Zenith." Pivoting, she set the Stetson on the hood and dug into her briefcase. "Harvey entrusted me to deliver this to you."

Opening the envelope she handed him, Clint inspected the generous cheque and folded it into his jeans pocket. When all was said and done, he should have a nice little nest egg left over. "Thanks."

"Now you can take your ranch off the market."

He shook his head. "Tia and I have decided to move."

Sonya blinked back the tears of regret that filmed her eyes. "It's all because of me, isn't it?"

Rock nodded. "We want you to coordinate a publicity campaign for us."

He didn't want her, only her expertise. Her heart plummeted. "The one you mentioned on the radio."

"Yeah. We're relocating to Toronto to be near you."

"You'd leave all of this—" she gestured to the ranch, and the majestic mountains beyond "—for me?"

Rock's gaze devoured her. "When I moved here, I told myself I wanted to provide Tia with a stable lifestyle, to give her roots, and I did. Witnessing your struggle to come to terms with your past gave me the courage to address my own. My own roots had been planted in guilt. You helped me accept that I couldn't have prevented what happened to Kristin. You've also helped me realize Tia isn't like Kristin." He tucked his thumbs in the loops of his jeans and surveyed his property. "Yes, I love this land—it's a part of me. But it's not more important than people. It's not more important than you."

A tear slipped down her face. "I'm important...to you?"

He cradled her face in his hands. "You're way beyond important. I love you, Sonya."

Her heart blossomed with ecstasy at the magic of his words. "I love you, Rock," she breathed.

Lowering his head, he brushed her lips with his, before returning to claim them with exquisite tenderness. Suffused with exhilaration, Sonya wrapped her arms around his neck and abandoned herself to his touch.

A lifetime later, with her still locked in his embrace and nestled against his heart, he whispered, "I can't let you go, Sonya. So we'll follow you."

"Well, you won't have to travel far. I'm staying right in Calgary." She looked up and grinned at the surprise on his face. "Harvey has retained Duncan and Associates to handle the Rocky Ridge campaign."

He gave her a seductive smile. "Any chance of me being hired as a model?"

Turning in his arms, she reached into her briefcase and handed him the second envelope. "You're our first, and only, choice."

Glancing at the envelope containing the contract, he reclaimed her eyes. "I don't need to read it. I'll accept—on one condition."

"Name it."

An intense green light glowed in his eyes. "Agree to marry me."

She pursed her lips. "It's tempting. But I have a couple of conditions, too."

"Such as?"

"One, you take the ranch off the market."

"Done. What's the second?"

She picked up the Stetson and placed it on her head. "Kiss me, cowboy."

He smiled. "With pleasure, ma'am."

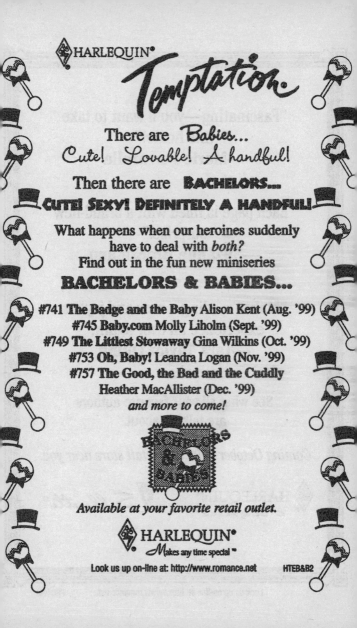

COMING NEXT MONTH

#745 BABY.COM Molly Liholm
Bachelors & Babies

When bachelor Sam Evans finds a baby on his doorstep he's surprised. Little Juliette even comes with a web page and care instructions! *Then* Anne Logan appears on Sam's doorstep. The sexy nanny agrees to help, but soon she doesn't know *who* is more trouble—the teething tot or lovesick Sam!

#746 A CLASS ACT Pamela Burford
15ᵗʰ Anniversary Celebration!

Voted "Most Likely To...Succeed," lawyer Gabe Moreau has done exactly that. But he's never forgotten gorgeous Dena Devlin. Time hasn't erased the hurt...or the hot sizzling attraction between them. Their high school reunion will be the perfect place to reignite those feelings....

#747 NIGHT WHISPERS Leslie Kelly

DJ Kelsey Logan knows what she wants—stuffy but sexy Mitch Wymore. So what if the handsome prof doesn't care for her late-night radio venue "Night Whispers"! It's a show about romance and fantasy—two things Kelsey is absolutely convinced Mitch needs in his life....

#748 THE SEDUCTION OF SYDNEY Jamie Denton
Blaze

Sydney Travers's biological clock is ticking loudly, but there's no suitable daddy in sight. Except Derek Buchanan, who is her best friend and *hardly* lover material. But Sydney has no idea the sexy scientist is in love with her—and determined to seduce Sydney at the first opportunity.

**Starting in September 1999,
Harlequin Temptation®
will also be celebrating
an anniversary—15 years
of bringing you the
best in passion.**

**Look for these
Harlequin Temptation® titles
at your favorite retail stores
in September:**

CLASS ACT
by Pamela Burford

BABY.COM
by Molly Liholm

NIGHT WHISPERS
by Leslie Kelly

THE SEDUCTION OF SYDNEY
by Jamie Denton